HONKERS UNDER THE HOLLY
THE COCKY KINGMANS

AMY AWARD

Copyright © 2024 by Amy Award

All rights reserved.

No part of this book may be reproduced in any form or by any electronic or mechanical means, including information storage and retrieval systems, without written permission from the author, except for the use of brief quotations in a book review.

Art by Gonda

Cover Design by Jacqueline Sweet

HONKERS UNDER THE HOLLY

What happens when a struggling sports agent and a plus-size model fake an engagement to save a rescue goose? Christmas chaos, that's what.

I didn't plan to pretend to be in love with the gorgeous plus size model who rescued a goose from the chopping block at Oktoberfest. But when Sir Honksalot destroys her apartment and my parents sell their shop right before Christmas, a fake engagement seems like the perfect solution to our mutual housing woes.

Now we're house-sitting a mansion together, but confined to one room...with only one bed. We have to convince everyone we're the most boring couple in L.A., while dealing with a delinquent waterfowl with a sock-stealing habit and feelings that don't feel fake at all.

This curvy girl romance features a bad-tempered rescue goose with his own social media following, a sports agent who's secretly a romantic at heart, and a baddie plus-size model who knows her worth – all set in a prequel to the everyone's favorite football family, the Kingmans.

CONTENT NOTE

This is a book of fluff. Fluff I pulled out of my butt...no that doesn't sound right. I just mean that I had no idea this little piece of joy was inside of me until I decided to write a holiday novella at the very last minute. So I'm very proud of this particular piece of fluff, because it came at a time in the world when we need fluff, and joy, and hope.

This fluffy story is meant for escapism and laughs. We need fluff; it's the insulation from the harsh world around us.

But just because this is a light-hearted holiday novella, doesn't mean there isn't conflict. The characters in this book face some bigotry in the form of fatphobia and homophobia. There is also references to the loss of a friend who was a mother. If you need to skip those chapters, just know, everyone gets a happy ever after. Even the goose. I love to write about funny animals and pets. No pets will ever be harmed or die in any of my books.

What I can promise you though is that my books will always hold a space that is free of physical violence against women including sexual assault. That just doesn't exist in the world I create in my mind.

I like to cry at touching Super Bowl commercials, not in my romances.

wink

I wrote this so you can swoon, and giggle, and kick your feet, and find some joy. But I also wrote it to help you (and me) escape the real world chaos for just a little while so we can rest up to continue our battles.

P.S. - I know I took liberties with the way photoshoots for magazines work. But it wouldn't have been as much fun to have our characters do their jobs in a timely manner, in a studio, in... I don't know... August. So, just go with it, and have some fun.

For everyone who needs a love story to reminds us joy exists even in chaos.
I'll be your safe space when you need it, so you can escape, rest, and rejuvenate for when it's time to get back out there and continue the fight.

If you feel the urge, don't be afraid to go on a wild goose chase. What do you think wild geese are for anyway?

— WILL RODGERS

A WILD GOOSE CHASE

I weaved through the crowded Oktoberfest tent, the scent of bratwurst and sauerkraut mingling with the crisp October air. My phone buzzed in my pocket for the third time in ten minutes. I didn't need to look at it to know it was Tommy "The Tank" Wilson, my only signed client and the reason I was navigating this sea of lederhosen and dirndls on a Friday night.

"*Entschuldigung*," I muttered, squeezing past a group of rosy-cheeked revelers. My high school German teacher would've been proud. Or maybe not, considering I was pretty sure I'd just apologized to a wooden support beam.

I spotted Tommy at a long table near the back, already three steins deep if the empty glasses in front of him were any indication. So much for our "quick meeting to discuss strategy." The guy was built like a brick house but had the alcohol tolerance of a gnat.

"Mac, my man!" Tommy's voice boomed through the tent as I approached. He raised his current stein, sloshing beer all over the already sticky table. "Have a seat! Have a beer!"

And this was why Tommy was a free agent with no prospects. Which made me a sports agent with even fewer prospects.

I slid onto the bench across from him, plastering on my best "responsible agent" smile. "Hey, Tommy. How about we talk about that offer from the Razorbacks? The coaching staff have a position—"

"Razorbacks, schmazorbacks," Tommy slurred, waving a hand dismissively. "Tonight, we celebrate! Prost!"

He clinked his stein against an imaginary glass in front of me and took a long swig. I watched, a knot forming in my stomach. This was the guy I was pinning my fledgling sports agency on? The guy who was more interested in setting records for beer consumption than rushing yards? The Bandits had won their Thursday night game against the Mustangs despite Tommy acting more like a lump on a log than a running back. If he wasn't one of my best friends…, but he was and that meant something.

A waitress appeared at my elbow, her blonde braids swinging as she set down another stein and some delicious-looking apple strudel in front of Tommy.

"Anything for you, sir?" she asked, her German accent as thick as the foam on the beer.

I looked up, ready to decline, not really into the fake milk maid thing, but the words died in my throat. Her blue eyes sparkled with amusement, and a dimple appeared in her cheek as she smiled. She was tall, and lush, with an ass that was barely covered by the floofy skirt and even more curves in all the right places. Her dirndl hugged her thick figure in a way that made my mouth go dry.

"I, uh..." Real smooth, Mac. I cleared my throat and tried again. "I'll have some of that strudel and a water, please. Someone's got to be responsible here."

She laughed, and the sound had my heart do a little polka. "Very responsible. I'll be right back with that."

She walked away, and I couldn't help but watch each sway of those hips. Tommy, despite his inebriated state, noticed. He let out a low whistle. "Now that's what I call a first and ass."

That didn't even make sense. I turned to him, ready to steer the conversation to his career, but he was already halfway through his new stein. This was going to be a long night.

My phone buzzed again, this time with a text from my mom.

> Got another offer on the shop today. Your father's excited. Don't forget to start packing. Smiley face.

She hadn't quite learned to use actual emojis in her texts yet.

Great. Just awesome. Not only was my sole client more interested in partying than playing, but I was about to be homeless. Some sports agent I was turning out to be.

The waitress returned with my strudel and water, setting it down with a wink. "Enjoy, Mr. Responsible."

I grinned despite myself. "Thanks, Ms...?"

No ring, so yes... yes, I was fishing. She was definitely the best part of this evening.

"Sara," she supplied with a cheeky grin. She knew exactly what I was asking. "Sara Jayne Bauer."

"Mac Jerry," I replied, extending my hand. She shook it, her grip firm and warm.

A crash from across the tent drew her attention. "Ach, duty calls. Perhaps I'll see you later, Mac. *Prost.*"

As she hurried off to deal with whatever drunken disaster had just occurred, I turned back to Tommy, determined to salvage something from this meeting. But he was face-down on the table, snoring softly...like a gnat.

I sighed, fishing out my wallet to pay. Some third-round draft pick he was turning out to be. At this rate, I'd be living in a cardboard box behind my parents' soon to be sold sports memorabilia shop before I ever saw a decent commission.

I looked around, hoping Miss Sara Jayne was still nearby to settle Tommy's tab, wincing knowing the total would be ridiculous. But a commotion erupted near the entrance of the tent. Raised voices and startled yelps punctuated the usual Oktoberfest cacophony.

"Komm zurück, du dummer Vogel!"

I turned to see a blur of white feathers zip past, followed by a flash of blonde braids and blue dirndl. Sara Jayne, her face flushed and hair escaping its neat plaits, was in hot pursuit of what appeared to be... a goose?

The bird honked indignantly, weaving between legs and tables with surprising agility for something that looked like an angry pillow with a beak. Sara was close behind, muttering what I assumed were German curses under her breath.

Without thinking, I stepped into the aisle, arms

outstretched, despite the twinge in my bum shoulder. "I got it."

The goose, apparently not impressed by my heroic stance, darted between my legs and made a beeline for Tommy's table. In a move that would have made any football coach proud, it leapt onto the bench and used Tommy's broad, unconscious back as a springboard, launching itself toward freedom.

"Oh no, you don't," I growled, lunging after it. My fingers closed around nothing but air as the goose banked hard right, letting out a triumphant honk.

Sara skidded to a stop beside me, cheeks pink from exertion. "He's heading for the beer."

Sure enough, the feathered menace was making a dash for the row of tapped kegs along the back wall. Foamy beer geysers and angry German brewmasters was not a scenario I wanted to face.

"Not on my watch," I muttered, breaking into a run.

I vaulted over a table, scattering pretzels and narrowly avoiding a face-full of brats and sauerkraut. The goose was just yards from the kegs now, its webbed feet slapping against the sawdust-covered floor.

With a desperate dive that would have made Tommy proud, if he were conscious, I launched myself forward. Visions of my second to last play in my senior year of college in the championship game flashed through my mind as I sailed through the air, arms outstretched, fingers grasping.

Then, contact. My hands closed around a warm, feathery body just as I crashed to the ground, sliding the final few feet on my good arm, to bump gently against the kegs.

"Gotcha," I wheezed, tightening my grip on the squirming goose.

Cheers erupted inside the tent. I rolled onto my back, holding the indignant bird against my chest, and found myself looking up into Sara Jayne's beaming face.

"*Mein Held!*" she exclaimed, dropping to her knees beside me. Before I could process what was happening, she cupped my cheeks in her hands and planted a kiss squarely on my lips.

For a moment, I forgot about everything—the goose, the crowd, even the fact that I was lying on a beer-soaked dirt floor. Sara Jayne's lips were soft and warm, and tasted faintly of cinnamon and something uniquely her. I returned that kiss, one hand still firmly grasping the goose while the other found its way to the back of her neck and then into her hair.

When we finally broke apart, both a little breathless, reality came crashing down in the form of an angry honk from the bundle of feathers on my chest.

Sara Jayne's eyes widened, but there was a sparkle in them, and a blush flashed across her cheeks. "Oh, sorry, I got carried away, I—"

The way she stifled a giggle, she wasn't one bit sorry, and neither was I.

I grinned up at her, feeling more alive than I had in months, maybe years. "For a kiss like that, I'd happily offer my goose-catching services anytime you need them."

She laughed, the sound sending a warm tingle down my spine. Then she focused on our new feathered friend, her expression softening. "Oh, you poor thing. Don't worry, you're safe now."

I sat up, still holding the bird. "And why did I just tackle this fine piece of poultry? What are we saving it from?"

Sara Jayne bit her lip, a mix of embarrassment and determination crossing her face. "I may have... liberated him from the catering company's pen out back. They were going to..." She drew a finger across her throat.

"Ah," I nodded, looking down at the goose. It glared back at me with one beady eye. "Well, congratulations, buddy. You just got a stay of execution."

Sara Jayne beamed at me, and I felt my heart do that odd little polka again. "Thank you so much for your help, Mac. I don't know what I would have done if he'd gotten away."

I carefully transferred the goose to her arms, trying to ignore the disappointment running through my skin as she moved back. "Always happy to help damsels and waterfowl in distress. Although," I glanced around at the mess of scattered food and spilled beer, "I'm not sure the festival organizers will be as understanding about your jailbreak."

She made that oh-shit grimace. "*Scheiße.* Yeah. I'm pretty confident I'm fired. I just couldn't bear the thought of this little guy ending up on someone's plate. Hopefully, this is a golden egg laying goose and will help me manifest a new job."

The goose honked. It had better be laying her a dozen golden eggs for the way she just forfeited her job for its life.

I stood up, brushing sawdust from my clothes, and held out a hand to help her up. "Tell you what. Why don't we get this guy somewhere safe, and then I'll help you smooth things over with your boss? I can be very persuasive when I need to be."

Sara Jayne took my hand, juggling the goose as she got to her feet. "Why would you do that? You barely know me."

I shrugged, feeling a grin tug at the corners of my mouth. "I'm a sucker for a pretty girl with a kind heart. And, well, I've already got one challenging client to manage. What's one more?"

"Client? Are you a lawyer?"

"Sports agent." I jerked my thumb over my shoulder at Tommy. "The tank over there is my guy."

She laughed, adjusting her hold on the goose. "Alright, Mr. Sports Agent. Lead the way. But fair warning, if you thought chasing a goose was tough, wait until you try explaining this to Helga."

After some smooth talking and a promise for tickets to the next Bandits game to make up for the Great Goose Chase, I managed to convince Helga not to fire Sara Jayne. The festival manager's scowl softened slightly when she saw how gently Sara Jayne cradled the goose, muttering soothing words in German. She'd transformed that angry bird into a puddle of love goo. Did birds purr?

"Fine," Helga grunted. "But that *Ringelgans* cannot stay here. It goes, or you both go. *Verstanden?*"

Sara Jayne nodded vigorously. "*Ja, natürlich.* Thank you, Helga."

Helga stomped away, and Sara turned to me, her blue

eyes shining so brightly I nearly got lost in the glow. "I can't believe you did that. You're amazing, Mac."

Something tingled in my chest and it had nothing to do with the beer I hadn't drunk. "Hey, it's what I do. Well, usually with fewer feathers involved, but..."

She laughed, then glanced down at the goose in her arms. "I should probably get this little *Süßer* somewhere safe. My shift ended during all the excitement."

"Need a lift?" The words were out of my mouth before I could think twice. "I mean, as soon as my big guy's ride picks him up, I'm headed out anyway. Tommy's's, uh, down for the count." I jerked a thumb towards my friend, who was still snoring face-down at his table. His dude-bro teammates would be here to get him in a few minutes, in the limo I was providing as incentive.

Sara hesitated for a moment, then nodded. "That would be wonderful, actually. If you're sure it's not too much trouble?"

"Trouble? Nah. Although," I eyed the goose warily, "if he poops in my car, you're on clean-up duty."

The ride to Sara Jayne's apartment was... interesting. The goose had strong opinions about my taste in music. Every time I tried to put on some classic rock, he'd honk loudly until I changed it. When I landed on a pop station, this apparently met with His Feathered Majesty's approval. His head literally bopped to "Baby Got Back."

"Okay, Sir Honksalot, I see you." I winked at Sara Jayne. "I also like when she's got buns, hun."

"Oh my gawd. I'm definitely naming him Sir Honksalot. Way better than Goosy McGooseface, which is what I was originally thinking."

As we pulled up to her building, I couldn't help but feel a twinge of disappointment. I wasn't ready for this bizarre but wonderful evening to end.

Sara Jayne must have sensed my hesitation. "Would you like to come up? I mean, just to make sure Sir Honksalot settles in okay. And maybe for a nightcap? To thank you properly for everything?"

My heart and my cock did a little victory dance. "I'd like that."

The apartment was small and a bit chaotic, filled with mismatched furniture and the chatter of several girls getting ready for a night out. Sara Jayne introduced me and Sir Honksalot to her roommates, who were less than thrilled about their new feathered friend.

"Sara Jayne, honey, you can't keep bringing home strays," one of them sighed, eyeing the goose warily. "Last month it was the ugliest kitten I've ever seen, and that thousand year old hamster or gerbil or whatever."

Sara Jayne's face fell, and she hugged the goose closer. "It was a hedgehog. But Sir Honksalot is different. I can't just take him to the shelter. He only needs a temporary home until I can find a farm animal sanctuary or something."

The other girls left, all three of them giving Sara Jayne and her strays, me included in that, the side-eye.

Sara Jayne created a makeshift pen she conjured up with couch cushions and a towel. Who took so much care and compassion with an animal well known to be a murder bird? But the way it clearly already loved her, this girl was something special.

"Okay, so I may have exaggerated about that night cap.

I've got water or... and don't knock it till you try it, pickle juice."

"I'll stick with the water."

We talked for hours, long after her roommates had left. Sara Jayne told me about her struggles to make it as a plus-size model in a size-zero world. I shared my dreams of building a successful sports agency. I kept my fears now that my parents were selling their shop, and my apartment along with it a little closer to the chest.

I'd never had a more intimate night without anything more than the touch of fingers when she handed me drinks.

As the first light of dawn started to creep through the windows, Sara Jayne stifled a yawn. "Oh wow, I can't believe how late it is. Or rather early? But I won't say I'm sorry for keeping you up all night."

I grinned, leaned in, and cupped her cheek. "Best night I've had in a long time."

Even if it had gone very differently from any other evening I'd spent with a woman. While I wanted to kiss her again, badly, wanted to do a whole lot more with her too, I also didn't want to ruin this magic spell she'd somehow cast over me. It was the worst timing. My life was up in the air, I only had half a fledgling career, and not a lot of prospects. But I liked this girl, more than I should, and I wanted more with her than some one-night stand.

"I'm gonna head out. Let you get your beauty sleep."

She blinked at me and something flashed through her eyes, but she nodded and stood up, stretching.

She walked me to the door, a soft smile on her face. "Thank you again, Mac. For everything."

"Anytime," I replied, meaning it more than I'd ever meant anything in my life.

Just as I was about to leave, a loud honk came from the living room, followed by the sound of flapping wings and a crash.

Sara Jayne's eyes widened in panic. "Oh no, Sir Honksalot."

We rushed back to find the goose had somehow escaped his pen and was now proudly perched atop the TV, which was upside down with a shattered screen.

Of course, that was the exact moment Sara Jayne's roommates got home. They took in the scene, and the one who'd chastised her before fixed Sara Jayne with a steely glare. "That's it. The goose goes, or you do. You have until the end of the week to decide."

The roommate slammed her door shut, and Sara turned to me, her eyes filling with tears. "Oh Mac, I can't abandon Sir Honksalot, but no way will I ever be able to afford to move out on my own. I'm barely getting enough gigs to keep up with the rent of this place."

I looked at Sara Jayne, then at Sir Honksalot, who seemed far too pleased with himself, and a crazy idea formed in my sleep deprived brain. "I might have a solution. Hear me out."

A MODEL DILEMMA

The incessant honking pierced through my dreams, dragging me back to consciousness. I blinked, disoriented, as sunlight streamed through the blurry curtains. What time was it?

I sat up, rubbing my eyes. "I'm coming, Sir Honksalot. Keep your feathers on."

As if on cue, another honk echoed through the apartment, followed by an aggravated groan from the next room. Right. My roommates. Who were probably plotting goose-icide at this very moment. None of us were early risers, but thank goodness Honksalot had woken me up before noon. I had an appointment at the agency this afternoon.

I padded into the living room to find Sir Honksalot parading around his cushion fort, head held high like he owned the place. Which, given the events of last night, he kind of did.

"Good morning, Your Honkness," I said, scooping him up. He nuzzled into my neck, surprisingly affectionate for a bird I'd known less than twenty-four hours. "Let's get you some brunch before the natives revolt."

I rummaged through the lackluster fridge contents looking for a meal to prepare for both Sir Honksalots and me. Our choices were salad or salad. Sigh. What did everyone have against carbs? "Kale or cabbage, buddy?"

The goose eyed the salad suspiciously before deigning to take a bite. As he munched, I leaned against the counter. I'd much rather be hanging out with Mac again than what I had to do today. Mac's strong arms holding my rescue goose... and me. Kissing like that one last night. The hours we spent talking...

Sir Honksalot flung a piece of kale at my face. He was way more excited about greens than I was.

His potential solution was as intriguing as it was vague. What could a sports agent's client possibly do with a goose? Start a water polo team?

I shook my head. "We can't pin all our hopes on a guy we just met, Honksy. No matter how impressive his... problem-solving skills are."

Sir Honksalot made a soft snuffling sound, almost as if he was agreeing with me... or he was just enjoying his food. I really needed to make some friends who weren't of the avian variety.

"But it's not like I know what I'm going to do with you. You got any ideas?" I asked him, stroking his feathers.

He responded with one loud honk, then turning his attention back to his breakfast.

A door slammed, jolting us both from our breakfast. My roommate Zoe stormed into the kitchen, her face a thundercloud.

"Sara Jayne," she said, her voice dangerously calm. "Why is there a goose eating my organic kale?"

I glanced down. Sir Honksalot had his beak buried in the bowl of fancy greens. "Um... he has expensive organic taste?"

Zoe was not amused. "This isn't funny, Sara Jayne. That bird has to go. Do you know how much noise he made this morning while we were all trying to sleep? I have a big shoot today, and I'm gonna look like the marshmallow man sat on my face."

"I'm sorry, Zoe. I'll find him a new home, I promise. I just need a little time." Or for a particularly sexy sports agent to come to our rescue, again.

She crossed her arms. "There are plenty of models, who are actually working and can pay their rent on time who would love to take your half of that room. You have until Friday. After that, it's you or the goose."

As Zoe stomped out, I slumped against the counter. "Ooph. I think we're both in the doghouse. Or goose-house, as the case may be."

I glanced at the clock. Zoe wasn't wrong about me not working. I was hoping my meeting with the Elite One agency owner today would change that. One could not live on Oktoberfest tips alone. Especially since this was the last week. "Okay, Your Honkness, change of plans. You're coming with me to my room while I get ready. Tessa's away on assignment, so you'll have the place to yourself while I'm at the agency."

Sir Honksalot seemed perfectly content with this arrangement, especially when I turned on some music. Classic Whitney Houston played, and he began to bob his head in time with the music, his whole body swaying.

"Oh my god," I laughed. "You really are something else, but I can't blame you. We all wanna dance with somebody."

The agency was bustling when I arrived, models and photographers rushing about in controlled chaos. I made my way to Magda's office, my portfolio clutched tightly to my chest. She'd had me do some new shoots in hopes of attracting new interest.

I was really hoping the fact that she'd called me to a meeting meant that this was it. My chance to finally book a real job.

Magda looked up as I entered, her sharp eyes taking in every detail of my appearance. "Ah, Sara Jayne. Come in and close the door, please."

I perched on the edge of the chair across from her desk, trying to project confidence I didn't feel. "Thank you for seeing me, Magda. I have those new photos—"

"Sara Jayne," she interrupted, holding up a hand. "Yes, I've seen them, and they're good. But we need to discuss your progress. Or rather, the lack thereof."

My heart sank right through my stomach and dropped to the floor. This wasn't about a new job. "Okay. What can I do?"

Magda sighed, taking off her glasses. "It's been six months since we signed you. In that time, you've booked exactly two jobs. Both local, both low-paying. We need to strategize."

"I've been doing everything my agent asks," I offered,

but she understood that. I didn't know what else to do. "I've been to every casting call, every—"

"I know," Magda cut in. "Your work ethic isn't the issue. The fact is, the plus-size market is... challenging. Especially here in L.A. We might need to consider some alternative markets."

I tensed, sensing where this was going. She didn't mean back to Germany. "What kind of alternative markets?"

Magda hesitated, then said, "We've had some interest from weight loss companies. They're always looking for 'before' models, and—"

"No," I said firmly, cutting her off. "Absolutely not. I won't do weight loss ads."

"Sara Jayne, be reasonable. It could be a good opportunity to be seen."

"April De la Reine has never settled, never let the industry dictate her career, even through seven pregnancies," I said, my voice rising. "And I won't either. I'm here to be a fashion model, not to perpetuate harmful stereotypes."

Magda held up her hands in surrender. "Alright, alright. I understand. And between you and me, I respect your stance. I'm a fan of April's work too. Not just in modeling, but in body positivity. Lord knows our industry could use some of that." She leaned back in her chair, considering me. "But we need to do something to boost your visibility. Have you considered social media?"

I blinked, thrown by the change in direction. "Social media?"

"Yes. There's this up-and-coming thing called InstaSnap. It's all the rage with the younger crowd, and since it's amazing pictures and videos, it's perfect for our industry. If you could build a following there, showcase your personality along with your modeling... it could open up a lot of doors."

I nodded slowly, bringing things together, everything whirling in my mind. "I could do that. Sir Honks—I mean, I have some ideas that could be interesting."

Magda raised an eyebrow but didn't comment about my near slip. "Good. Work on that. In the meantime, I'll keep pushing for fashion bookings and look into some networking opportunities for you."

She paused, thinking for a moment, then added, "Actually, my husband and I are having a holiday party next week at my estate. You haven't been out yet, but we do a lot of photoshoots there and I like to entertain."

She gave me a once up and down look as if evaluating what she wanted to say next. "Why don't you come? It could be good for you to meet some potential clients and industry people in a more relaxed setting. Of course, there are Jones's football buddies too, so you might bring a date if you don't want them all over you."

Holy *Hagebuttenmark*. An invitation to one of Magda's parties was usually reserved for models at the agency at the top of their game. If she wanted me to come, she must really believe in my potential. I was blown away by the offer.

"Thank you, yes. I'll be there. Thank you." I sounded like a fool, but I couldn't get over the invite. Maybe I really could get my foot in the door and get some jobs. And if I could get jobs it meant other little girls around the world who 'had a pretty face' or 'would be so pretty if they'd just lose a few pounds' might just feel seen too.

I left Magda's office, my head was spinning with everything we'd discussed. An InstaSnap account. A holiday party. But still no solid bookings.

My phone buzzed with a text. It was from Mac.

> Can't stop thinking about last night. And this morning. And Sir Honksalot's dance moves. Coffee later? I might have some news about our feathered friend.

A smile spread across my face as I typed my reply.

> Me too. Pick a place where we can talk about unconventional pet care without people thinking we're crazy.

> Challenge accepted. How about the cat cafe near the pier? If they can handle cats, they can handle talk of a rap-loving goose.

I laughed out loud, earning curious looks from the other people in the elevator. I didn't care. For the first time in months, I felt a glimmer of hope. And not just for my career, but my love life too. It had been as stale as my booking prospects ever since I came to the United States. American men were just not the same as German ones.

I practically skipped the entire way home, my mind buzzing with possibilities. Maybe I could feature Sir Honksalot in my InstaSnap posts. A plus-size model with a rescue goose? That had to be a unique angle, right?

I was so lost in my thoughts that I almost missed the

commotion coming from my apartment as I approached the door. Frowning, I quickened my pace and fumbled with my keys.

I swung the door open and was greeted by a scene of utter chaos. Feathers floated through the air like snow. The contents of my closet seemed to have exploded across the living room. And there, in the middle of it all, stood Sir Honksalot, looking entirely too pleased with himself.

In his beak dangled the mangled remains of what had once been my favorite pair of Jimmy Choo pumps.

"Sir Honksalot," I gasped, horrified. "What have you done?"

He dropped the shoe and let out a triumphant honk, as if to say, "I've redecorated. You're welcome."

I sank to my knees, surveying the damage. I was so lucky the rest of the girls weren't home. How had he even gotten out of my room? As I picked up a tattered blouse, a glint of metal caught my eye. There, hidden beneath a pile of destroyed clothing, was a bent hairpin.

"You picked the lock?" I asked incredulously. "With a hairpin? Should I have named you Goosedini?"

Sir Honksalot just waddled over and nestled against my leg, looking up at me with what I swore was a mischievous glint in his eyes. He was so cuddly and I couldn't stay mad at him.

I sighed, giving his feathers a gentle stroke. "You're lucky you're cute, you know that? Now, what am I going to wear for my coffee date with Mac?"

As if in response, Sir Honksalot waddled over to the chaos and pulled out a simple, yet elegant sundress I'd forgotten I owned. It had survived the goose massacre unscathed.

I couldn't help but laugh. "Are you my stylist now, too? Fine, I'll wear it. But this doesn't get you off the hook for the shoes, mister."

I made Honksy a new couch cushion fort and began the daunting task of cleaning up. It was mostly clutter, and I got most of it swept up and all but my clothes put away by the time my phone buzzed again. Another text from Mac.

> Great call with my client. Might have that solution for our feathered friend. Can't wait to tell you over coffee. See you soon.

I looked at Sir Honksalot, who was now contentedly preening himself amidst the wreckage of my wardrobe. There was no way I could leave him here alone again. Not if I wanted to have any clothes left, or roommates.

"Looks like you're coming with me, Your Honkness," I sighed, eyeing him warily as I changed into the sundress he'd "picked out" for me. "Let's hope this cat cafe is open-minded about their clientele."

I managed to fashion a makeshift carrier out of a large tote bag, lining it with a soft blanket. Sir Honksalot, surprisingly, seemed quite content with this arrangement, settling in with only minimal fuss.

As I approached the cafe, I could see Mac through the window, already seated at a table sipping on a mug of something with, oh my, was that a plate of glazed *Lebkuchen* in the shape of cats? My heart did a little flip. Had he ordered those for me?

No, no. Couldn't be. Anyone would order gingery-goodness shaped cat cookies in a cat cafe. This was about Sir Honksalot. He was just being a really nice guy.

That I definitely had an enormous crush on.

The bell above the door jingled as I entered and Mac looked up. His grin went wide, then shifted to confusion as he noticed the large, oddly shaped bag I was carrying with a feathered head sticking out the top.

"Sara Jayne, you look... um, really beautiful, drool-worthy honestly," he said, standing to greet me. Then, glancing at my bag, "Is that...?"

I nodded, setting the bag gently on an empty chair. "I couldn't leave him alone after what he did to my closet. I hope that's okay?"

Mac laughed, his eyes twinkling. "Of course. Though I'm not sure how the cats will feel about it."

As if on cue, Sir Honksalot let out a honk like he was also saying hello. Several nearby cats perked up their ears, looking around in confusion.

"Maybe we should move to a table outside," Mac suggested, already gathering his things, and the plate of cookies. "Give His Honkness some privacy."

Once we were settled in a spot on their deck area, I carefully let Sir Honksalot out of the bag. He looked around with interest, seemingly unfazed by the feline presence inside the cafe.

"So," I said, trying to keep my voice casual, like this was just business. Because if I didn't I was going to do something impulsive, like kiss him again. "You mentioned you might have a solution to my pet problem?"

Mac nodded, leaning in conspiratorially. "Okay, hear

me out. Remember Tommy, my slightly inebriated client from Oktoberfest?"

I nodded. "Of course. But I'm not sure I like where I think you're going with this."

"I swear he's actually a good guy. He's just kind of let the money go to his head. He's in a little of a wild child phase." He broke off a bit of one of the cookies and dropped it for Honksy. The goose hustled toward the treat. But the moment he sniffed at it, he turned up his nose at it. "Well, I convinced him he needs to improve his image if he wants to stay with the team. And I had this crazy idea—what if he became the proud owner of a slightly quirky pet goose?"

My eyes widened. "You mean Sir Honksalot?"

"Exactly," Mac grinned. "Plus, we'd set Tommy up with a shiny new InstaSnap account to document his adventures with his unique pet, and get him to hire a professional pet wrangler to help him. It could be great PR for him and a home for loosey goosy here."

I took a cookie from the plate and took a bite mostly to hide the stupid happy smile breaking out on my face. He'd thought of everything, and I didn't think it was because he was a huge goose lover. "That's... actually kind of brilliant. And weirdly coincidental. My agent just told me I need to start an InstaSnap account too."

Mac's eyebrows shot up. "Really? That's perfect. We could collaborate on content. The sexy plus-size model and the football player, united by their love for a dancing goose. It's social media gold."

Tommy, the beer-guzzling football player was not the

one I wanted to be united in love with. Not... that I was in love. Lust, though? Yes, absolutely.

As excited as I was about the idea, a small worry nagged at me. "But what about Sir Honksalot? Is Tommy ready for full-time pet ownership, even with a pet wrangler?"

Mac's smile faltered slightly. "That's the thing. I'm not entirely sure he is. I was hoping maybe we could work out some kind of... joint custody?"

The words were out of my mouth before I could stop them. "Joint custody? You mean, between you and me?"

Mac's cheeks reddened slightly. "Well, no. But I'd be, uh, the custody liaison, if you're okay with that. And, you know, it would give us a reason to keep seeing each other regularly."

Oh, we didn't need a reason beyond this delicious attraction between us, but the fact that he wanted one, had manufactured this whole scenario, gave me all the warm tinglies in my belly.

"I'd like that," I said softly. Then, just to play along, I added, "For Sir Honksalot's sake, of course."

"Of course," Mac agreed, a twinkle in his eye.

Our new shared custody goose must have been very excited about this arrangement because he flapped his wings and jumped right up on my back. Which sent me tumbling forward, knocking over the cookies, our drinks, the table, and everything.

But that dang bird wasn't done. When Mac and I stood trying to avoid the destruction, Sir Honksalot came at Mac, and knocked him right into me. We went down, in a tangle of limbs, me right on my ass, and Mac... well, he ended up face first in my lap.

Then, as if nothing happened, Sir Honksalot waddled over to the cookie crumbs and started pecking at them, like they were a reward for a job well done.

Mac slowly raised his head, his eyes following the line of my exposed thigh. He eventually ran out of leg and managed to look up at me. The way his eyes twinkled at me had my panties immediately on fire.

He licked his lips and grinned up at me. "Well, wasn't that a wild ride?"

Why did I have a feeling that was less of a question and more of a promise? I sure hoped so.

EVERYONE LOVES AN UNDERGOOSE STORY

I'd seen some bizarre contract negotiations in my day—okay, that's a lie. Outside of law school, I'd seen exactly two contract negotiations. The first when I signed Tommy to SMTM Sports Management two and a half years ago, and the second when I got him signed to the Bandits. But this definitely topped that.

My tiny home office, usually reserved for obsessively refreshing my email inbox hoping for potential client inquiries, now hosted a very different kind of meeting. Tommy sprawled across my secondhand leather couch, still in his L.A. Bandits practice gear, while Sara Jayne perched on my desk chair. Sir Honksalot waddled between us, systematically destroying my last remaining business cards.

"So let me get this straight," Tommy said, his attention torn between scrolling on his phone and Sir Honksalot. "You want me to share custody of a pet goose? Like, an actual goose?"

"Sir Honksalot isn't just any goose," Sara Jayne replied,

her voice carrying that warmth that was sweet, caring, and turned me the fuck on. "He's a rescue with special needs. And right now, those needs include a yard, which you have, and I don't."

I cleared my throat, switching into what I liked to call my agent voice. "This is an opportunity for some image rehabilitation, Tommy. You need some good press before the upcoming contract negotiations. That unfortunate karaoke incident at The Tipsy Pickle didn't help."

Tommy winced. We all winced. Even Sir Honksalot seemed to shudder at the inherent awfulness of Tommy's tone-deaf rendition of Happy Birthday—to himself—while standing on the bar in nothing but his practice shorts, one sock, and a half dressed ball bunny who he clearly couldn't care less about.

"The public loves a personal growth story," I continued, pulling this pitch out of my butt. "League football player takes in rescued waterfowl? That's pure gold. We could have you trending for something positive for once."

Sir Honksalot chose that moment to demonstrate his approval—or possibly his disdain—by snatching Tommy's phone off the couch and taking off down the hallway at a speedy waddle.

Man, that goose could move. I should sign him to my SMTM's sports management roster.

"Hey," Tommy yelped and jumped up. "That's a brand new iPhone."

"You're going to scare him if you chase him," Sara Jayne shouted, but it was too late. Tommy was already in pursuit, his years of training weirdly working against him as Sir Honksalot led him on a merry chase through my parents' kitchen.

Mom stuck her head out from behind the curtain that separated the shop from our living space. "Everything okay up here, Maguire, sweetheart?"

"Fine, Mom. Just a little fowl situation." I called back, then turned to Sara Jayne. "Well, at least they're bonding?"

The crash from the kitchen suggested otherwise.

"I got him." Tommy's voice carried through the house. "And he only cracked the screen a little."

Sara Jayne smiled and shook her head. Then she pulled up InstaSnap on her phone. "So, I've already started building Sir Honksalot's social presence. He's got five thousand followers just from the Oktoberfest videos."

I leaned over her shoulder, trying to focus on the phone and not how good her shampoo smelled, or the way her tits seemed to be calling to me to press my face between them. Shit. That wasn't a very gentlemanly thing to think. We weren't going to make any progress if all I could focus on was her... nope, stop that right now.

I dragged my eyes back to the screen. The latest post showed Sir Honksalot wrapped in a tiny knitted scarf, looking surprisingly dapper for a honking menace. The caption read: "Looking for my forever home(s)! This special goose needs special arrangements. Stay tuned for a big announcement! #RescueGoose #SirHonksalot"

"This could actually work." If I could get Tommy's reputation out of the shitter, and make him a media darling, I might be able to make this dream of being a big-time sports agent a reality.

My mom called up to my office again. The first thing I

was doing as soon as I got my percentage of Tommy's new contract, was buying my parents that house they wanted in Florida.

"Maguire, honey, can you come down to the shop when you're done? Your father and I need to discuss something with you."

I knew that tone. That was the same tone she'd used when she told me my goldfish had "gone to live in a bigger pond" when I was six.

"Everything okay?" Sara Jayne asked.

"Yeah, just...you know," I gestured vaguely. "Parent stuff. Look, why don't you and Tommy work on the social media strategy while I deal with this? We can figure out the custody schedule after."

Tommy returned, phone clutched protectively to his chest, Sir Honksalot waddling smugly behind him. "Did someone say social media? Because I have some ideas involving tiny footballs."

I left them brainstorming and headed downstairs to the shop, trying to ignore the knot in my stomach. The bell above the door chimed as I entered Jerry's Sports Memorabilia, the same sound I'd been hearing since I was tall enough to reach the door handle.

Mom and Dad waited behind the counter where they'd been buying and selling players cards, balls, and jersey's and anything else with a signature for the past thirty years. The smell of leather and old paper wrapped around me like a familiar hug, but something felt off.

They were both smiling, but it was their nervous smile —the one they'd worn when they told me they'd "temporarily" converted my childhood bedroom into my home office six years ago when I left for college.

"Sit down, Maguire," Dad said, patting the old stool behind the counter.

I sat, feeling like I was a kid again and about to be grounded for using some official Harlem Globetrotters basketballs as bathtub toys.

"We've had an offer on the shop," Mom said, reaching for Dad's hand. "A very, very good offer."

The knot in my stomach turned to rocks, filled with lead. "What kind of offer?"

"The kind that would let us finally retire," Dad said. "Buy that little place in Florida we've been eyeing."

"Florida?" The word came out as a squeak. "But..."

I was hoping I'd be the one to retire them. "When?"

"Right before Christmas," Mom said softly. "We'd close the shop, pack up, and be moved in time to have a palm tree for Christmas."

The bell above the shop door chimed again, and Sara Jayne's voice floated down. "Mac? You might want to come back up. Tommy's teaching Sir Honksalot to catch, and I don't think it's going well."

I stared at my parents, then at the worn wooden floors I'd learned to walk on, then at the walls that had sheltered me my entire life. "Right before Christmas," I repeated. "As in, six weeks from now?"

Mom squeezed my hand. "We know it's sudden, honey. But you're a successful sports agent now. You can afford your own place."

I thought about my one client, my dwindling savings,

and the current state of LA's rental market. Success was a strong word for my career trajectory.

Another crash echoed from upstairs, followed by Tommy's voice: "It's cool. You needed a new lamp anyway, right?"

"I should..." I gestured toward the ceiling.

"Of course, honey," Mom said. "We can talk about all the plans to pack up more later."

I headed back upstairs, my mind spinning. Six weeks. I had Six weeks to figure out how to afford a place in LA's ridiculous housing market, or I'd be homeless just in time for the new year.

The scene in my office temporarily distracted me from my impending housing crisis. Tommy stood on my desk chair, holding a mini football over his head, while Sir Honksalot honked menacingly from atop my filing cabinet. Sara Jayne filmed the whole thing on her phone, providing commentary.

"And here we see the beginning of a beautiful friendship," she narrated. "Or possibly the start of a hostage situation. Stay tuned to find out! #FootballPlayerMeetsGoose #UnlikelyFriends"

Oh, god. Was this my life now? Mac Jerry, struggling sports agent, soon-to-be homeless, and now, apparently, goose custody mediator. If anyone had told me this would be my holiday season, I'd have asked what they were drinking and requested a double.

Two hours and seventeen takes later, we finally had something InstaSnap-worthy. Tommy sat cross-legged on my office floor, Sir Honksalot nestled surprisingly peacefully in his lap, both of them wearing L.A. Bandits caps that Tommy had signed.

"And that's why Sir Honksalot, Sara Jayne, and I are teaming up to raise awareness for animal rescue organizations," Tommy read from the cue card I held up. "Because everyone deserves a second chance—even if they're a little different, a little messy, or sing karaoke very, very badly."

Sir Honksalot honked right on cue, and Sara Jayne handed me the phone. "Follow us on InstaSnap and stay tuned for our first fundraiser. Can you say Bandit signed ball cap?"

She nodded at me and I stopped recording.

"That's was great. Magda was right about InstaSnap being a great way to get some notice. I can't do that at a photoshoot."

I handed the phone back to her, and she clicked away, posting the video. When she was done, she looked up at me and smiled, so happy and carefree. God, she was beautiful.

I wanted to cross the three feet between us and pull her into my arms. I'd dip her in that classic way and give her a long, deep celebratory kiss.

"Honk."

That was Tommy, and he was staring deep into Sir Honksalot's eyes. This looked like the beginning of a beautiful friendship indeed.

The phone dinged in Sara Jayne's hand. Then it did it again, and then it blew up with incoming notifications. She glanced down and her eyes went as wide as basketballs. "Whoa. They weren't wrong when they said this

InstaSnap was the next big thing. We've already had a couple thousand views and hundreds of hearts. It's only been three minutes."

"That's fantastic." I was trying to focus on work instead of the fact that I'd be sleeping in my car by Christmas.

Sara Jayne refreshed the page on her tablet. "The teaser posts from earlier today have already gotten ten thousand hearts. I didn't even know there were that many people on this media picture sharing thing. Magda's going to be thrilled—she's been pushing me to build a bigger social presence. Says the plus-size market is all about engagement these days." She trailed off, frowning at her screen. "Oh wow, speaking of Magda..."

She turned the tablet toward me. There, right under our post, was one from Magda Krol, owner of the Elite One modeling agency.

It was a picture of her and her husband hanging up some twinkle lights over the doorway to their McMansion. The caption read: Annual Fall Holiday Bash next Friday! Celebrating another year of breaking boundaries and making headlines. Special guests include models, football players, including Denver State's legendary Coach Bridger Kingman and supermodel April de la Reine! #ModelLife #FootballRoyalty #HolidaySeasonBegins

My heart did a little flip. Bridger Kingman wasn't just any college coach—he'd led the Denver State Dragons football team to three national championships in the past five years, and his DSU youth development camps had become the pipeline for top college recruits. His eldest son Chris was already being called the next great quarterback prospect...at twelve.. If I could just get my foot in the door with anyone in their world, it would be literally life changing.

"You should come with me," Sara Jayne said, as if reading my mind. "Magda's parties are legendary. Everyone who's anyone in L.A. shows up." She tucked a strand of hair behind her ear. "Plus, she specifically told me to bring a date. Says the football crowd can get a little... enthusiastic when they see a beautiful woman alone."

"You think I'm good holiday date material?" I tried to sound casual, not pathetically hopeful.

"Well, you did help me catch a rogue goose at Oktoberfest." She smiled. "And Magda's husband Jones played pro ball—apparently he and Coach Kingman go way back. Could be good for your agency to make those connections."

Tommy looked between us, grinning. "Oh, he'll be great at connections. He's been practicing connecting with—ow!" He rubbed his shin where I'd kicked him.

Sir Honksalot chose that moment to snatch Tommy's phone again and made a break for it.

Tommy bolted after him, his voice echoing down the hallway. "Come back here, you feathered menace!"

Suddenly alone with Sara Jayne, I noticed how the late afternoon sun caught the gold highlights in her hair. She fiddled with her phone, not quite meeting my eyes.

"You hesitated," she said softly. "When I mentioned the party. If you don't want to go—"

"No," the word came out too quickly, too eagerly. Real

smooth, Jerry. I took a breath and tried again. "I mean, I definitely want to go. With you. I just..." I ran a hand through my hair. "You're this amazing model who gets invited to fancy parties, and I'm just a guy who spent his morning reorganizing baseball cards in his parents' shop and making business plans on color-coded spreadsheets."

She looked up then, and something in her expression made my heart skip. "You know what I was thinking about during that whole photoshoot with Tommy and Sir Honksalot?"

"How my office needs redecorating?"

"How you didn't hesitate at all at Oktoberfest, or to help me find a home for Sir Honksalot, or... anything else that needs to be helped or fixed." She took a step closer. "When I went off acting before thinking, trying to catch a runaway goose, you just... jumped right in."

"To be fair, you're pretty impossible to say no to."

"And now?" Her voice was barely a whisper.

Instead of answering, I closed the distance between us and kissed her like I'd been wanting to for the past hour. Her lips were soft, tasting faintly of sweet lip gloss, and when I cupped her face in my hands, she made this tiny sound that nearly undid me completely. She wound her arms around my neck, pressing closer, and for a moment I forgot about everything—my housing crisis, the party, my struggling agency—everything except how perfectly she fit against me.

A loud honk and Tommy's yelped "Ouch," from the hallway broke the spell. Sara Jayne pulled back slightly, her cheeks flushed, but she didn't unwrap her arms from my neck.

"So," she said, a smile playing at her lips, "that's a definite yes to being my date?"

"That's a definite yes to everything," I murmured, stealing one more quick kiss before Tommy returned, rubbing his ass, with a smirking goose trailing behind. Did geese smirk? This one did.

"Great." Sara Jayne's smile did funny things to my chest. "It's at Magda's estate in Beverly Hills. Very fancy, lots of important people." She gathered up her things, then paused. "I can't believe April de la Reine will be there. Magda said they met when April was about to give up on modeling. She took some kind of vacation to Colorado, and the rest is history, I guess. Well, history and seven kids."

"A football player and a super-model," I repeated, my mind spinning with possibilities. "That's quite a power couple."

"Magda says April's been looking for fresh faces for her new clothing line's campaign." Sara Jayne bit her lip. "And Coach Kingman's youth development camps are renowned for finding amazing up-and-coming talent."

"Dude!" Tommy interrupted, finally retrieving his cap from Sir Honksalot. "This is perfect! You can pitch yourself as Chris's future agent while Sara Jayne networks with April. It's like... destiny, or whatever."

"When did you become such a smarty smartpants?" I asked.

"Since Sir Honksalot taught me the power of the sneak attack strategy." Tommy cradled the goose, who looked suspiciously smug. "And speaking of strategy, you better figure out what you're wearing because Magda's parties are legendary fashion fiestas. Last year's theme was 'Winter Wonderland' and someone showed up riding a real reindeer."

I made a face at him like I he was some kind of circus clown who'd just popped out of a car the size of his ass. "Wait, you've been to these?"

"Yeah." He shrugged. "Jones is my godfather."

I gaped at him. Why did I not know he was related to the most legendary tight end in Bandit history? All I knew about was how cruddy his parents were.

Sara Jayne nodded. "This year it's 'Hollywood Holiday.' Very glamorous, very festive." She gave me a quick once-over that made my ears burn. "Need help shopping?"

"He needs help everything-ing," Tommy muttered. "You should see his closet. Oh wait, you can't, because he's losing it."

"What?" Sara Jayne turned to me, frowning.

I shot Tommy a look that promised revenge, possibly involving Sir Honksalot and his favorite shoes. "It's nothing. Just... my parents are selling the shop. And the apartment above it. Before Christmas."

"Before Christmas?" Sara Jayne's eyes widened. "But that's less than six weeks away. Where will you go?"

"There's always Sir Honksalot's luxury doghouse," Tommy offered. "He's got that heating lamp and everything."

"I'm not living in a goose house," I said for what felt like the hundredth time.

"Just trying to help, man." Tommy settled Sir Honksalot more comfortably in his arms. "But seriously, something will work out. I mean, you're going to a fancy party with a beautiful woman, meeting Coach Kingman and a bunch of models. That's got to be a good sign, right?"

I watched as Sir Honksalot nestled contentedly against Tommy's Bandits jersey, looking like he'd been attending football practices as an emotional support goose his whole life. Maybe Tommy was right. Maybe this party was exactly what we both needed—Sara Jayne's chance to break into the big leagues of plus-size modeling, and my shot at proving I could handle a star prospect like Chris Kingman.

Or maybe we were about to humiliate ourselves in front of L.A.'s sports and fashion elite while wearing something "Hollywood Holiday festive."

Either way, at least we'd be doing it together. And right now, that made even the prospect of homelessness seem a little less terrifying. Though I was definitely drawing the line at the goose house. A man had to have some standards, even in a housing crisis.

FAKE IT TILL YOU MAKE IT

The moment our car pulled up to Magda's Bel Air estate, I knew I was in trouble. Not because of the red carpet entrance, or the champagne-wielding waiters in tuxedos, or even the actual searchlights sweeping across the night sky. No, I was in trouble because Mac Jerry, wearing a vintage-inspired tuxedo and nervously adjusting his bow tie, looked exactly like a 1940s movie star who'd stepped off the silver screen.

"You okay?" he asked, offering his arm as I carefully maneuvered out of the car in my gold lamé gown. "You seem tense."

"Just channeling my inner Rita Hayworth," I said, trying to sound more confident than I felt. The dress was a miracle find from a vintage plus-size boutique, and I'd spent an hour watching YouTube tutorials to get my hair into these perfect victory rolls. But it wasn't just the party and the deliciousness of being on Mac's arm making my stomach flutter.

This morning, my roommate Tiffany had cornered me

in the kitchen of our shared West Hollywood flat. "You're not fooling anyone, SJ," she'd said, examining her manicure. "We all know you're hiding that weird bird in your room. We told you, either the goose goes, or you do. Last warning."

Five models sharing a flat had seemed like such a good idea when I moved here six months ago. Now it felt like a shark tank, except with better cheekbone contouring.

"Is that Magda?" Mac squinted at a figure descending the grand staircase.

It was indeed Magda, my career fairy godmother, wearing what had to be vintage Valentino and dripping with old Hollywood glamour. She'd taken a chance on me when every other agency said plus-size girls were trending down. Now I just had to prove her right.

"Sara Jayne," Magda air-kissed both my cheeks. "That dress is perfection. And this must be the famous Mac. I've been watching those viral videos with Sir Honksalot. Brilliant campaign strategy."

"Oh, that was all Tommy and Sara Jayne's idea," Mac said, doing that adorable thing where he deflected praise. "I just try to keep the goose from eating the furniture."

"Too modest." Magda linked her arm through mine. "Sara Jayne, darling, April de la Reine has been asking about you. She loved the Oktoberfest rescue story. Come, I'll introduce you." She paused, glancing at Mac. "You don't mind if I steal her for a moment?"

"Of course not," Mac said, though his smile looked a bit strained. "I'll just... mingle."

I watched him head toward a cluster of men in tuxedos, walking like he was trying to remember which fork to use first at a fancy dinner. But the moment he infiltrated the circle of men, he received hand shakes and pats on the back like he was already one of the pack. Good, that meant I didn't need to rescue him and this was my chance—April de la Reine could change everything for me. Maybe enough to afford my own place, one where Sir Honksalot would be welcome.

"Now then," Magda said as we climbed the stairs, "let me tell you exactly why April asked about you. It seems her new line at Crown of Curves needs some fresh faces..."

I took one last look at Mac over my shoulder. He caught my eye and gave me a tiny wave that made my heart flip. Somehow, in the middle of all this old Hollywood glamour, that awkward little gesture felt more real than all the sparkle and shine combined.

April de la Reine was nothing like I expected. Oh, she looked exactly like her billboards—stunning, confident, curvy in all the right places—but she laughed like a college girl and kept stealing appetizers off her husband's plate.

"The Sir Honksalot videos are genius," she said, tucking a bacon-wrapped date into her clutch... for later? "That's exactly what we need for the Luxe Curve lingerie launch—authentic moments, genuine relationships. Not just posed perfection."

I tried to focus on her words—this was my big break, after all—but my eyes kept drifting to where Mac stood with a group of football players. I'd expected him to be awkward around all these ultra rich celebrity sports guys, but instead he was gesturing animatedly while the others nodded.

"Your young man played ball, didn't he?" April followed my gaze.

Coach Kingman - Bridger - nodded. "I recognized him right away. He had this fourth-quarter comeback in Oregon's last championship bowl game. Was one of the best throws I've ever seen. Too bad about his arm and knee. He might have been one of the greatest quarterbacks in the League."

My heart did a little skip. I knew Mac was a football fan, but he'd never mentioned being a player, or a career-ending injury.

Magda's voice drifted through the nearby French doors, sharp with frustration. "What do you mean Janet and Francois cancelled? They've watched the house for the holidays for the last three years."

I wasn't exactly eavesdropping, because she was having a meltdown twenty feet away in clear view of everyone in the room.

"No. No. It's six weeks in Europe and the Amalfi coast. Jones already booked the yacht." Magda paced the terrace, phone pressed to her ear. "The house is fully booked for photo shoots over the holidays. Who am I going to get? Who can we get on such short notice? This is a disaster."

Jones's attention turned from the circle of guys and he moved out to the terrace with his wife. He lay a calming hand on her shoulder. "We'll find someone, honey. What about one of your girls?"

"Are you insane? They're wonderful models, but... remember what I was like at their age? All parties and drama until I met you. We need someone stable. Boring, even. I want a nice, settled couple who'd rather organize their sock drawer than throw a rager."

I thought about my perfectly color-coded sock drawer. About Sir Honksalot, who needed a real home with a real yard. But I wasn't part of some boring settled couple. Unless...

Sometimes the craziest ideas are the ones that make the most sense.

"Excuse me," I said to April, already moving toward Mac. He looked up as I approached, his face lighting up in a way that made my impulsive plan feel a little less insane.

"Sara Jayne," one of the other players called out. "Jerry here was just telling us about the goose rescue. Man's got game—on and off the field."

Mac's ears turned pink. "I was just explaining how Sir Honksalot's social media presence could help shift public perception of Tommy's... enthusiasm for fun."

He looked so adorably professional, and smart, and not at all boring. Before I could overthink it, I grabbed his hand.

"Sorry to interrupt, but I need to borrow my fiancé for a moment."

Mac's eyebrows shot up, but bless him, he didn't miss a beat. Just squeezed my hand and smiled that smile that made my knees wobble.

"Of course, honey."

As I pulled him away, I whispered, "I need you to trust me and play along, okay? I'll explain everything later."

Because if we could sell this, in the next two minutes before Magda's assistant could come up with a solution, I think I could just solve both our housing slash pet goose problems.

"Does it involve a goose house? Because Tommy keeps sending me listings…"

"Even better." I took a deep breath.

I practically dragged Mac toward where Magda and Jake stood on the terrace, my heart pounding louder than the jazz quartet playing inside. This was either brilliant or career suicide. Possibly both.

"Magda," my voice came out an octave higher than intended. "I couldn't help but overhear—"

"Darling, eavesdropping is so gauche," Magda said, but she was smiling. She knew she'd been freaking out in front of a lot of her guests.

"—and I just, well, my fiancé Mac and I are exactly what you're looking for."

Mac's hand tightened on mine. I could practically feel him trying to figure out what he was supposedly perfect for.

"You are?" Magda's perfectly groomed eyebrows arched.

"We're literally the most boring couple in L.A.," I babbled. "Last Saturday night we spent three hours organizing his sports memorabilia by team, year, and player stats."

I hoped that made sense, because I had no idea if what I'd said even made sense, or that he wouldn't mind that I made that up right out of my butt.

"After alphabetizing her portfolio by clothing type," Mac added smoothly, catching on that whatever this was, it involved proving our boringness. God, I could kiss him.

Later. After he forgave me for whatever this was about to become.

"And the weekend before that?" I squeezed his hand.

"Comparison shopping for goose-safe cleaning products," he said, not missing a beat. "Had to make spreadsheets."

Jones laughed. "Sounds like you two are either perfect for each other or sharing a single personality."

"How long have you been engaged?" Magda asked. She was probably wondering why I hadn't mentioned it to her or had a ring on my finger. I needed to think fast.

I felt Mac's tiny jerk of surprise, but he covered it by pulling me closer.

"Not long," he said, which was technically true, since it had been approximately forty-five seconds. "I know I should have waited to get my grandmother's ring to ask, but I didn't want to wait."

Whoa, he'd even covered why I wasn't wearing a ring. He was anything but boring. In fact, his fast thinking was quite the turn on.

"It feels like we've known each other forever," I added, which was also true, even if we'd only met at Oktoberfest.

Magda studied us, head tilted. "And you're living...?"

"You know the girls at the flat aren't exactly goose-friendly," I blurted out.

"I was just telling Sara Jayne," April said, appearing beside us with a fancy bottle of water in one hand and several more bacon-wrapped dates in the other. "They have that natural chemistry you can't fake. Did you know Mac gave up a career in professional football and started his own sports agency just so he could help other players make it to the big time? That's the kind of stability you're looking for, Magda."

I looked at Mac, surprised. He hadn't told me that was why he'd become an agent. His ears turned pink again, but he held my gaze with a softness that made my chest tight.

"The guest house has a perfect yard for our bright, new celebrity Sir Honksalot," Jones mused. "You should sign him to your roster, sweetheart."

"You're serious?" Magda looked between us. "About house-sitting?"

"Completely," I said, then rushed ahead before I lost my nerve. "We're both at turning points in our careers, trying to be taken seriously. The last thing we want is parties or drama. Just a quiet place to build our future together." I looked up at Mac, silently pleading with him to back my play. "Right, honey?"

He brushed a kiss against my temple, so tenderly it almost felt real. "Nothing would make me happier."

Magda threw up her hands. "Jones, darling, call my assistant back and tell her we found someone. Sara Jayne, I'll have her draw up the paperwork tomorrow." She narrowed her eyes. "But if I come back to find my mother's vase in pieces..."

"The only parties we'll be having will involve spreadsheets and color-coding," Mac promised.

As Magda and Jake moved away to handle the details, I finally dared to look at Mac properly. "I can explain?"

His lips twitched. "So, about that future we're building together..."

"They needed boring, responsible people, and we're

the most well, we're kind of responsible people, aren't we? Plus, you need a place to live, I need a place for Sir Honksalot, and..." I bit my lip. "Are you mad?"

"Mad?" He grinned. "I just got engaged to the most beautiful woman at the party. Though we might need to discuss your definition of boring, because I'm pretty sure spontaneously fake-engaging yourself to someone counts as adventure sports."

The rest of the party passed in a blur of increasingly elaborate stories about our boring lifestyle. By the time we made it out of the party, I'd convinced half of L.A.'s elite that Mac and I spent our date nights comparing tax software, and he'd somehow worked our mutual passion for proper document filing into every conversation.

"I particularly enjoyed the story about our first kiss happening over a shared label maker," I said as we slid into the back seat of our the car Magda provided to take us home.

"Hey, that could have happened." He caught my hand, his thumb tracing circles on my palm. "Though I think I prefer the real version."

The memory of that kiss in his office made my cheeks warm. "Mac, about all this... I know it's crazy—"

"Sara Jayne." He turned to face me, his expression serious but soft. "You just solved both our housing problems, saved Sir Honksalot from eviction, and somehow managed to make my complete inability to be cool work in my favor. You're either a genius or completely insane, and I'm good with either option."

"Maybe a little of both?" I leaned my head against his shoulder. "I mean, what kind of person pretends to be engaged to someone they've only been dating for two weeks?"

"The kind of person who jumps into the beer-soaked fray at Oktoberfest to rescue a stranger's goose?"

"Fair point."

My phone buzzed with a text from Tommy.

> Just heard the "news" from three different people. Congrats on the engagement, you crazy kids. Sir Honksalot says it's about time.

The message was accompanied by a photo of our goose wearing a bowtie that perfectly matched Mac's.

Mac peered at the screen. "Should we be worried that Tommy's spending his Saturday night dressing up our goose instead of at the actual party with us?"

"Our goose?" I looked up at him.

His ears turned pink, and he gave me the cutest slightly sheepish smile that made my insides go a little squishy. "Well, we are engaged now. What's mine is yours, including joint custody of a partially reformed delinquent waterfowl."

I couldn't help it, I started giggling. After a moment, Mac joined in, and soon we were both laughing so hard the driver probably thought we were crazy. Maybe we were.

"Six weeks," I managed finally, wiping tears from my eyes. "In a mansion."

"With a goose." Mac was trying to hold back his laugh, but it came out as a snort.

"During the holidays." I giggled at him, at the ridiculousness of the situation, and the way the butterflies were tickling my stomach, my nerves, and maybe even my heart.

We looked at each other, and I felt that same flutter in my chest I'd gotten the first time he smiled at me.

"We are so not boring," I whispered.

He pulled me closer, and just before his lips met mine, he whispered back, "Don't tell Magda."

PLAYING HOUSE

"Son, that better not be the Manniway rookie jersey you're stuffing in there." Dad's voice carried from behind a tower of boxes. "That needs proper archival packaging."

I pulled the jersey back out of the moving box, trying to remember which of the seventeen different tissue paper colors Mom had designated for premium items. The shop looked strange all cleaned up of personal items, the display cases empty except for the last few items they'd be taking to the Florida house. Thirty years of sports history, all going into boxes or already sold to the new owner.

"Got the bubble wrap for the signed footballs," Tommy announced, bursting through the door with Sir Honksalot waddling importantly behind him. "And Sir Honksalot brought his organizational expertise."

"By which you mean he's going to steal things and hide them in random boxes?" I asked.

"Hey, his chaos has a system." Tommy dropped the

bubble wrap on the counter. "Speaking of systems, how's the move to the love nest—ow!" He rubbed his shin where I'd kicked him.

Dad emerged from behind the boxes. "You found a place, son? Why is it a love nest?"

"Just house-sitting," I said quickly, shooting Tommy a warning look. "For a client. Well, sort of a client. It's a networking thing."

"That's wonderful," Mom called from the back room. "Is it one of those football players you met? The ones from the party Sara Jayne took you to?"

"Yeah, Sara Jayne's boss and her husband are heading to Europe for a few months." I carefully didn't mention that Sara Jayne would be house-sitting too. Or that we were pretending to be engaged. Or that I couldn't stop thinking about how it didn't feel like pretending at all.

"Sara Jayne," Dad said thoughtfully, picking up a signed Mustangs helmet. "Sweet girl. Way too pretty for you."

I rolled my eyes. He wasn't wrong. She was hands down the most gorgeous woman I'd ever dated, or kissed, or been fake engaged to. "Thanks, Dad."

"No, I mean it as a compliment." He set the helmet in its designated box and winked at me. "The way she looks at you... reminds me of how your mother used to look at me when we were dating. Still does, sometimes, when she thinks I'm not paying attention."

Sir Honksalot chose that moment to snatch a Mountaineers pennant and take off toward the back room.

Tommy sprinted after the goose. "Sir Honksalot! We talked about this! Theft is not a personality trait!"

Dad chuckled. "Never thought I'd see the day when L.A.'s most promising running back was chasing a goose through my shop." He turned back to me. "You know, son, sometimes the best things in life come at you sideways. Your mother and I, we met when she accidentally sold her father's entire baseball card collection to me at a yard sale."

"I know, Dad. You tell that story every anniversary."

"My point is, don't overthink it. When something feels right..." He trailed off as a crash came from the back room, followed by Tommy's, "It's fine! Only knocked over the Bandits memorabilia."

Mom's voice rose in alarm. "Not the Bandits box. That's organized alphabetically."

I hurried toward the chaos, but Dad caught my arm. "Just... don't let a good thing slip away because of bad timing or circumstances like your parents up and selling your house out from under you. Sometimes life gets in the way, but when you know, you know."

The thing was, I did know.

Had known since Sara Jayne first smiled at me over a runaway goose at Oktoberfest. Everything since then, the social media scheme, the house-sitting arrangement, even this crazy fake engagement, it all felt like the universe's extremely unsubtle way of pushing us together.

Tommy returned with a smugly triumphant Sir Honksalot and a slightly crumpled pennant, "wait until you hear about the engage—"

"Engaging conversation we had about social media metrics," I interrupted. "Very boring. Lots of spreadsheets.

Hey, Tommy, didn't you want to show me that thing? Upstairs? Away from here?"

"What? Oh, right! The thing. With the... spreadsheets." He winked, so obviously I considered letting Sir Honksalot steal his phone again. Or his contract.

As I dragged Tommy toward the stairs, I heard Dad say to Mom, "Remember when we were that age and thought we were subtle?"

The next day, it felt very weird to show up with just a couple of duffle bags of stuff at the front door of the mansion I was going to call home for the next few weeks.

"Our master suite has the best morning light for shoots," Magda said, leading us through the rooms of the house. "I often use it when we're trying different lighting setups."

I hadn't realized that the house sitting would also involve people coming and going all the time. It meant a lot more work keeping up our fake engagement charade. No way I was letting Sara Jayne lose any of Magda's confidence in her because of reports that we weren't... I don't know, engaged-acting enough.

"These other rooms are all set up as styling stations and equipment storage," she explained. "The schedule for who is using which room and when is posted on the doors so no one disturbs anyone else's set up."

Sara Jayne and I exchanged a quick glance. We'd planned to take separate rooms—but it seemed like every one of the bedrooms, even in a house this size, were all going to be occupied with the modeling and photography business.

Magda continued her tour, breezing past closed doors

without opening them, and it would be way too risky to try to stay in any of them.

Sir Honksalot waddled past the French doors out in the garden, as if he'd already claimed the entire estate as his domain. Through the windows, I could see his luxury pet house being assembled by Jones's personal assistant. It had a fountain. An actual fountain.

This goose sure was good at winning hearts and minds.

"Now, the main house alarm codes," Magda continued, but I was distracted by Sara Jayne's subtle shifting beside me. She'd been quiet since we'd arrived, and I wondered if she was as overwhelmed by all of this as I was.

We'd been on exactly one and a half dates. While I'd spent plenty of time fantasizing about having her in my bed, I doubted either of us thought we'd actually be stuck with only one bed for the both of us like this.

A bed that, as we discovered when Magda threw open the double doors to the room that was designated as ours, dominated the room like a cruise ship had docked in a sea of sea-colored carpet.

The theme song from "The Love Boat" popped into my head.

"Brand new memory foam especially delivered for you two this morning," Magda said with a knowing smile that made my ears burn. "Jones insisted all the beds in the house be ultra-comfortable, supportive and durable."

She winked at Sara Jayne. "Have fun breaking it in."

Sara Jayne made a sound that might have been agreement or possibly just pure panic.

"I had everything in here reorganized last week, so

there's room for both your things. Though Sara Jayne, darling, we'll need to clear some space for the wardrobe from tomorrow's shoot." Magda said, checking her phone, which she grimaced at.

"Well, dears, it looks like you'll have to put up with Jones and I another two days. She showed us her phone briefly, not that I caught what was on the screen. But Sara Jayne's eyes went wide. "Illustrated Sports just won't wait for me to get back from the Amalfi coast to wrap up casting."

She typed something, sending off a rapid fire message, then looked at me. "You don't happen to have any clients nearby that could do a test shoot at four, do you, Mac, darling?"

Did I? "Would an L.A. Bandits running back work?"

"Oh, perfect. I always forget Tommy is here. Sometimes it's hard for me to remember he's all grown up. Call him will you, while I break the news to Jones that we can't leave, at least until Monday." She air-kissed us both. "Don't worry about unpacking now. Plenty of time for that after the shoot!"

She swanned out, leaving us alone in what was apparently our bedroom. Our very much singular bedroom. With its very much singular bed.

"So," I said intelligently.

"So," Sara Jayne agreed.

From the garden, Sir Honksalot's triumphant honk suggested he'd discovered his fountain.

"I can sleep on the floor," I offered.

Sara Jayne turned to me, her expression fierce as she glanced down at my knee. At least, I think it was my knee she was looking at below my belt. "We're adults. We can share a bed for a little while without it being weird. Can't we?"

The problem was, everything about Sara Jayne made my pulse race in a decidedly non-platonic way. Sharing a bed, even just for sleep, seemed like an exercise in exquisite torture.

A hint of pink bloomed up her cheeks, and she looked at the doorway, lowering her voice to a whisper. "If Magda and Jones are here for two more days. We have to make this look convincing."

She was right. And I was in so much trouble.

A crash from the garden interrupted whatever I might have said. We rushed to the French doors to find Sir Honksalot had indeed discovered the fountain. He appeared to be teaching it who was boss.

"Well," Sara Jayne said, fighting a smile, "at least someone feels at home already."

I looked at her, hair falling loose from her braids, trying not to laugh at our goose's aquatic dominance display, and thought—*I'm already home. That's the problem.*

After a dinner where Jones regaled us with stories about his playing days while Magda continued to take calls about the model casting for Illustrated Sports, Sara Jayne and I found ourselves alone in our room. Our room. The phrase still made my pulse skip.

She stood at her suitcase, pajamas clutched to her chest. "I'll just..." She gestured toward the en suite bathroom.

"Right. Yes. Good idea." Smooth, Jerry. Real smooth.

While she changed, I tried not to think about the fact

that we'd be sleeping in the same bed. Instead, I focused on practical things. Like changing into my sleep pants and t-shirt. And wondering if I should have packed nicer pajamas than my old college sweatpants. And absolutely not thinking about how Sara Jayne's toothbrush was already on the bathroom counter, right next to mine, looking like they belonged there together.

She emerged in soft-looking pajamas of a tank top and shorts printed with little clouds, her face scrubbed free of makeup. She looked younger, softer somehow. And absolutely beautiful.

"Bathroom's free," she said, not quite meeting my eyes.

When I came out a few minutes later, she was perched on the edge of the bed, looking about as nervous as I felt.

"I really can take the floor," I offered, eyeing the vast expanse of carpet.

"Don't be ridiculous." She fixed me with that fierce look I was coming to know well. "You have an old injury, and that carpet isn't nearly as plush as it looks."

"It's not that bad—"

"Mac." She patted the space beside her. "We're both adults. And we need to make this look convincing for two more days. Come to bed."

The way she said it, so matter-of-fact yet slightly breathless, made my heart do complicated things.

I slid under the covers on the far side, trying to maintain a respectful distance without looking like I was avoiding her. The bed was enormous, but I swear I could feel the heat from her body across the space between us.

"This is weird, isn't it?" she whispered into the darkness after I'd turned off the lamp.

"Little bit."

"Should we like... talk about it?"

"The weirdness?"

"All of it." She shifted, and I could feel her looking at me even though I couldn't quite see her face. "The fake engagement that doesn't feel very fake. The way you smile at me when you think I'm not looking. The fact that I really want to move closer, but I'm afraid if I do, I won't want to move back."

My heart stopped. Then started again, double-time.

"Sara Jayne..."

She shifted closer, and I wanted to kiss her and touch her and spread her thighs, losing myself between them. But Sara Jayne moved first, putting herself right into my arms in a way that felt perfectly natural. Enough that when my arm ended up around her, it didn't feel like crossing a line.

She fit perfectly against me, her head tucking under my chin like it was made to rest there. Her hair smelled like vanilla and something floral, and I tried very hard not to think about how right this felt.

"Is this okay?" she whispered.

Did I want to fuck her? Yes, absolutely. But holding her like this was something almost more overwhelming than my need for her. I closed my eyes and let myself imagine more than just one night with her. I imagined years and years together. "Better than okay."

"Good." She yawned. "Because you're really comfortable. And warm."

I pressed a kiss to the top of her head before I could

overthink it. "Get some sleep. We have weeks to figure out the rest."

But as her breathing evened out, and she curled closer in her sleep, I wondered if maybe we'd already figured it out. Maybe we were just waiting for our hearts to catch up to what they'd known since that first day I saw her.

A quiet honk from the garden sounded suspiciously like approval.

I woke sometime in the night to find Sara Jayne had turned in my arms, her face now inches from mine. Moonlight filtered through the French doors, casting silver shadows across her features. One of her hands rested against my chest, right over my heart.

She must have felt my breathing change because her eyes fluttered open, meeting mine in the darkness. For a moment, neither of us moved.

"Hi," she whispered.

"Hi." My voice was rough with sleep.

Her fingers curled slightly against my t-shirt and her eyes sparkled in the night. "I meant what I said before. About this not feeling fake."

I reached up to brush a strand of hair from her face, letting my fingers trail along her cheek. She leaned into the touch, and something in my chest tightened. Other parts of me below the belt tightened too.

"None of it feels fake," I admitted. "Not since the day we met."

She shifted closer, erasing the last inches between us. "Mac?"

"Hmm?"

"Kiss me?"

Thank fuck. I cupped her face in my hand and brought my lips to hers. This wasn't like our previous kisses, playful after the party, sweet during our goose adventures. This was slow, deep, full of everything we hadn't been saying.

Sara Jayne made a soft sound and pressed closer, her hand sliding up to the nape of my neck. I traced the curve of her hip, then the dip at her waist, marveling at how perfectly she fit against me. When she gently bit my lower lip, I had to stifle a groan.

She pulled back just enough to meet my eyes, her breath warm against my lips. "I know this is all happening so fast..."

"Yeah," I agreed, though I couldn't stop my fingers from tracing patterns along the small of her back. God, I wanted her so badly.

"And we're still just getting to know each other..."

"True." I pressed a kiss to that spot below her ear that made her shiver.

"And we're living in someone else's house..."

"Also true." My hands found their way under the hem of her pajama top, skimming the soft skin of her waist.

She arched into my touch. "So, we should probably take this slow."

"Probably," I murmured against her neck. I could make incredibly slow, sensual love to her if she wanted me to.

"Be responsible adults."

"Absolutely." I captured her lips again, and for a few long moments, being responsible was the last thing on either of our minds.

Finally, Sara Jayne pulled back, her chest rising and falling rapidly. "Mac?"

"Mm?"

"We're not being very responsible."

Dammit. I pressed my forehead to hers, trying to catch my breath. If she wanted to put on the breaks, that was entirely her choice. I wanted nothing but enthusiastic consent from her. While I was absolutely sure I could push and end up with her under me, giving her orgasm after orgasm, I would wait until she wanted that as much as I did. "No, we're not."

She traced my bottom lip with her thumb. "I want this to be real. All of it. Not just because we're caught up in the moment or the pretense or—"

I kissed her softly, cutting off her words. "I want it to be real too. That's why I can wait." I smoothed her hair back from her face. "We have time."

She smiled that smile that had been undoing me since day one. "Six entire weeks."

"And after that?"

The way she smiled up at me, the way it made my heart forget how to do anything else but beat for her. I knew I was falling so fast and so hard for her, I would never get back up. "After that, we won't have to pretend we're pretending anymore."

She settled back against me, her head tucked under my chin, one leg tangled with mine. Her breathing slowly evened out, but I stayed awake a while longer, memorizing the feel of her in my arms.

Six weeks. Six weeks to turn this beautiful chaos into

something real. Into something that felt as right as holding her right now.

I was pretty sure we wouldn't need nearly that long.

SLIP A GOOSE UNDER THE TREE FOR ME

"*L*eft a bit. No, my left. The tree's left? Just... everyone stop moving."

I watched from the sidelines as Sun Chen, the legendary female photographer, tried to wrangle a six-foot-four hockey player, a willowy model, and a twelve-foot Christmas tree into the perfect holiday tableau.

Magda had called me a few days ago to emphasize how important this Illustrated Sports shoot was and asked if I would be onsite to make sure it went well. My job was supposedly just to be there to help in any way anyone needed. So far, that had mostly involved keeping Sir Honksalot from eating the artificial snow.

"Sara Jayne, sweetie," Sun called out. "Can you adjust Svetlana's hat? It's throwing shadows on her face."

I approached Svetlana, who perched on a ladder while wearing what had to be the shortest Mrs. Claus dress in history. She glared down at me like I might contaminate her with my plus-size cooties. She'd looked the same way at Sun, but had put on an excellent fake smile when she realized exactly how this shoot could make or break her career. Sun was that powerful.

"Don't mess up my hair," she snapped.

"Wouldn't dream of it." I reached up to tilt the fur-trimmed hat, catching Sun's approving wink in my peripheral vision. The photographer had made waves last year by refusing to Photoshop any of her subjects, claiming genuine beauty didn't need digital enhancement. The fashion world had been scandalized. Sun had been booked solid ever since.

"Much better," Sun adjusted her lens. "Now, Leo, honey, try to look less like you're planning to check Santa into the boards."

Leo Iverman, star goalie for the Denver Blizzard, grinned sheepishly. "Sorry. Force of habit."

"We want 'Sexy Santa,' not 'Santa's Going to the Penalty Box.'" Sun snapped a few photos and frowned down at her camera. Then she turned to me. "This isn't working for me. Something is just off about the whole shoot."

Uh-oh. That wasn't good. Magda wouldn't be happy if this photoshoot didn't go well and right now the look on Sun's face was looking like she was ready to throw in the towel. "How can I h--"

"Honk." I was definitely wishing Sir Honksalot hadn't chosen that moment to waddle past with one of Derek's hockey socks in his beak. Why did he love athletes' stinky feet so much?

Sun raised an eyebrow and her eyes sparkled with mischief. "That's what's missing. We've got sexy shirtless hockey Santa supposedly cozy at home before the holidays, and that should be whimsical, and this looks all too boring and like manufactured perfection."

I knew that tone. It was the same one everyone seemed to get around this crazy goose. "What did you have in mind?"

"I want to put the goose in."

"Oh no," Svetlana interrupted. "No birds. I don't do animals. What if it shits on me?"

"Perfect." Sun clapped her hands like it was a done deal. "That's exactly the energy we need. Get the goose."

Sir Honksalot, apparently believing his big break had finally arrived, decided to let everyone know he was ready for his close up. He honked at Svetlana, who screamed and toppled off her ladder. Leo, showing off those legendary goalie reflexes, dove to catch her. Unfortunately, his face met her elbow while her face met his shoulder, and suddenly we had two broken noses and no cover models.

"I'm calling my agent," Svetlana wailed through the ice pack the assistant had produced. Of course, her agent worked for Magda, so I was definitely getting a phone call momentarily.

"Not the first time or the last time breaking my nose," Leo mused, examining his reflection in a nearby ornament. "Very hockey player chic."

Sun lowered her camera, surveying the carnage of fallen garland and scattered artificial snow. "Chic, and honestly, kind of hot. But not what Illustrated Sports wants for the cover."

"Magda's going to kill me," I muttered. I guess Mac

and I should start packing now. I hoped Tommy was in town and not traveling for some away game and could take Sir Honksalot in. Otherwise, the three of us were going to be homeless. Nobody wanted a homeless goose on InstaSnap.

"Unless you've got another sports media darling hidden in your back pocket, we're going to have to cancel this shoot." Sun shrugged like this was no big deal to her.

"I have an idea."

From across the room, I caught Mac's eye. He'd been helping set up lighting all morning, and something about seeing him in jeans and a tool belt had been doing funny things to my insides. He raised an eyebrow in silent question.

Before I could respond, my phone buzzed with a text from Magda.

> Why is Svetlana's agent calling me about a rogue goose attack?

Sir Honksalot honked triumphantly from his new perch atop the Christmas tree, Leo's sock still clutched in his beak like a trophy.

"What do you mean you have an idea?" Sun asked, but not in an accusatory way. More like she was prompting me. Like... she'd planned this all along. Which was ridiculous.

"Mac is a sports agent, and I'm sure he's got a client that could hop in on short notice." Once again, I was praying Tommy was in town.

Sun nodded and was already striding toward Mac, her camera swinging from her neck.

HONKERS UNDER THE HOLLY

She pointed at Mac. "You're a sports agent? Who's on your roster?"

Mac nodded, clearly confused about why this mattered when we had a model storming out, a hockey player with a bloody nose, and a goose causing a lot of chaos.

"Tommy Frayzer, running back for the LA Bandits."

"Oh, yes, he's deliciously perfect. Illustrated Sports cover guy for sure. Call him," Sun commanded. "Get him here. Now."

I watched Mac's face transform as he caught on. "No problem. But don't you also need—"

"A Mrs. Claus," Sun finished, turning to me with a gleam in her eye. "Someone who knows how to work with Sir Honksalot. Someone real."

My stomach dropped, bounced like a red rubber ball, and went right up into my throat. "Why are you looking at me?"

Sun grinned. "You're perfect. The curves, the natural chemistry with the goose, the way you light up when Sports Agent Boy looks at you..."

I felt my cheeks heat. Was I that obvious?

"But I'm not cover model material... yet," I protested. "I mean, I am a model, but not for something this big. This is Illustrated Sports."

"Exactly." Sun was already moving, directing her assistants to adjust the lighting. "They want something fresh. Something authentic. Leo, honey, how's the nose?"

"Had worse, like in last season's playoff game," Leo called from where the medic was tending him. "Wanna come kiss it and make it all better for me?"

"Why are the hockey players such insufferable flirts?" Sun winked at him. "Don't go anywhere. I've got an idea for a naughty Jack Frost shoot that we'll get IS to use for their January issue."

I wanted to be like Sun Chen when I grew up. She was the mistress of her universe right now, and I was a little in awe.

"Sara Jayne, go see Paolo for wardrobe, hair, and makeup. Mac, get Tommy here in the next twenty minutes or I'm putting you in the Santa suit."

Mac was already on his phone. "Tommy? Drop everything and get to Magda's. No, you don't need to bring emergency tacos. Thanks for thinking of us, though."

"Are you sure about this? Will Illustrated Sports really put a plus-size model on the cov—" I started, but Sun cut me off.

"Look at me," she said, her tone gentler. "I've spent twenty years in this industry watching them try to force everyone into the same tiny box. But the genuine moments? The ones that make a cover pop? They happen when we let people be themselves."

She gestured to Sir Honksalot, who had finally descended from the tree and was now attempting to organize the scattered ornaments into some sort of pattern. Either that or he was eating them. "Even if themselves happen to include a slightly chaotic goose."

"Magda's going to freak out," I whispered.

"Magda," Sun said with absolute certainty, "is going to love it. Now go. Paolo's waiting, and we have a Christmas miracle to create."

As if on cue, Mac appeared at my side. "Tommy's on his way. You okay?"

I looked up at him, at the way his eyes crinkled with concern, at the faith there that made me believe anything was possible. "Yeah," I said, surprising myself by meaning it. "I think I am."

"Good." He squeezed my hand. "Because you're going to be amazing."

"Enough with the cute," Sun called out. "Save it for the camera. Paolo, we need her camera-ready in fifteen!"

As I let Paolo usher me toward the makeshift styling station, I glimpsed my reflection in one of the giant ornaments. I didn't look terrified anymore. I looked... excited. Ready.

Maybe Sun was right. Maybe the best moments really do happen when you stop pretending to be something you're not.

Though I was definitely going to need someone to explain to Magda how I'd just scored the cover of a sports magazine and why my goose was now on her modeling client list. But to be fair, he did look pretty sweet wearing tinsel like a feather boa.

"Trust me, give me five minutes with a needle and threat and this Mrs. Claus dress is going to fit you perfectly, doll." Paolo pulled at some material here, tugged at some there, and then stepped back to admire his handiwork. "A little sexy Mrs. Claus, a little old Hollywood glamour, and a lot of you."

He was right. The red velvet hugged my curves, strangling the girls just a little, but the way he'd used a bolt of white fur trim to make a plus-size dress out of something that barely fit a size zero fifteen minutes ago was nothing less than a miracle. I looked like a 1950s pin-up Mrs. Claus in the best possible way. My hair fell in soft waves, and he'd given me the kind of red lips that belonged on a Christmas card.

"Places, everyone," Sun called out. "Tommy, stop teaching the goose running plays."

"But he's really getting the hang of play-action passes," Tommy protested. He looked amazing in his Santa pants and suspenders, and about a thousand pack of abs. Though I noticed they'd let him wear his lucky Bandits socks—the ones Sir Honksalot was constantly trying to steal.

"The goose stays on his mark," Sun directed, adjusting her camera. "Sara Jayne, I want you by the fireplace. Tommy, casual lean on the mantel. Like you just came down the chimney to find sassy and sweet Mrs. Claus waiting for you after a long day of reindeer games."

I channeled my inner Rita Hayworth, and I took my position. From behind Sun's lighting setup, Mac gave me a thumbs up that somehow made me feel both more nervous and more confident.

"Perfect," Sun started shooting. "Now just talk to each other. Be natural. Forget I'm here."

"So," Tommy said, his eyes twinkling with mischief. "Come here often?"

I laughed despite myself. "Only when my goose crashes cover shoots."

"Speaking of..." Tommy nodded toward Sir Honksalot, who had positioned himself regally beside my skirts like some kind of waterfowl courtier. "Someone's working that tinsel."

"Beautiful," Sun called out. "The chemistry is perfect. Tommy, move closer. Sara Jayne, that laugh is everything. Sir Honksalot... actually, the goose is nailing it."

We fell into an easy rhythm, the conversation flowing naturally as Sun's camera clicked away. Tommy told me about his latest touchdown celebration, which apparently involved the Macarena. We were just normal people, co-parents to a goose, and friends, albeit dressed a little weird.

"Okay, now for the shot I've been waiting for." Sun lowered her camera. "Tommy, remember what we discussed?"

Tommy's grin turned downright devious. Before I could ask what they'd discussed, he dropped to one knee in front of me.

"Sara Jayne," he announced dramatically, holding up an enormous costume jewelry ring, "you've changed my life. No one else would help me teach a goose the importance of proper social media presence. No one else would risk their designer shoes to wade into a fountain after said goose. You're one of a kind."

I caught on to the game and pressed a hand to my heart. "Tommy, are you saying...?"

"Will you..." He paused for maximum effect. "Help me teach Sir Honksalot the Macarena?"

The entire room burst out laughing, including Sun, who was shooting rapidly to capture every moment. I smiled over at Mac, but he wasn't looking at me. He was...

scowling at Tommy? No, that must be his worried about what Sir Honksalot was going to do face.

"That's it," she exclaimed. "That's the cover! The realness, the joy... it's perfect."

Sir Honksalot chose that moment to snatch the ring and take off across the set.

"Should we stop him?" Tommy asked.

"Yes, chase him like the sexy running back that you are, Tommy," Sun ordered, still shooting. "This is gold."

I caught Mac's eye again as Tommy chased our goose around the Christmas tree. He was looking at me with something that made my heart flip, something that felt an awful lot like pride mixed with... more.

"And that's a wrap." Sun announced. "Someone catch that goose before he breaks anymore noses. I'd like to keep mine intact, thank you very much."

The house was quiet after the chaos of the day. I changed out of the Mrs. Claus dress, but kept the old Hollywood hair and red lips. Something about them made me feel brave. Beautiful.

"Sun sent over some preview shots," Mac said, joining me on the couch with his laptop. "Want to see?"

I curled into his side, breathing in his familiar scent. "Show me."

The first image took my breath away. Tommy and I were laughing at something, the Christmas lights creating a soft glow around us. But what caught my eye was how... real I looked. Happy. Like I completely belonged there.

"You're incredible," Mac said softly, his fingers tracing patterns on my bare shoulder.

"The styling team did a great job—"

"No." He set the laptop aside, turning to face me. "You. You're incredible. The way you handled everything today, how you just... shine, no matter what chaos is happening around you."

He cupped my face, thumb brushing my lower lip. "I need to tell you something."

My heart did a complicated gymnastics routine worthy of the seventy-six Olympics. "Okay..."

"I don't want to pretend anymore."

"Oh." My heart had a hard time finding the next beat. "The fake engagement, you mean. Right. Of course. We can—"

"No, Sara Jayne." He took my face in both hands. "I don't want to, can't pretend I'm not completely in love with you."

The world stopped. Started again. Stopped once more for good measure.

"You're what?"

"In love with you." He leaned closer, his breath warm against my lips. "I'm completely, head over heels—"

I cut him off with a kiss, pouring everything I couldn't say into it. His hands slid into my hair as he pulled me closer, and suddenly the pretense of the past weeks melted away. This was real. This was us.

"I'm in love with you too," I whispered against his mouth. "So much."

Our kisses grew more frantic and Mac drew me into his lap. I straddled him and traced the strong line of his jaw, his shoulders, remembering all the times I'd wanted to touch him like this but held back. Not anymore.

This day was crazy and chaotic, and somehow also

incredibly perfect. Knowing Mac loved me just made it all the better. It was like everything I'd ever wanted was coming to me all in one giant present of a day.

Mac's hands slid down my back, leaving trails of heat through the thin fabric of my camisole. He whispered against my neck. "I know we're taking it slow, but fuck you feel so good."

"I only wanted to take it slow because... I was worried you thought I was crazy for getting us into all of this. We'd only been on like one and a half dates before we moved in together." I ran my fingers through his hair, loving how he shivered at my touch.

"Sweetheart, I've been crazy for you since you asked me to trust you and announced our engagement. Probably even before that, if I'm being honest. Today... when Tommy got down on one knee, I almost jumped onto the set to punch him in the face."

"I'm sure that's supposed to be a red flag, but I'm finding it a ridiculous turn on that you wanted to beat someone else up over me."

He stood, lifting me with him like I weighed nothing. "Oh god, Mac, be careful. I don't want you to strain your knee injury."

Mac laughed and squeezed my butt. "I may not be able to play ball anymore, but I promise I can carry my girl to bed. Now wrap those long legs around my waist so I can take you to our bedroom and lay you on our bed.

And wasn't that a thought that made my heart race? Our bedroom.

No more pretending.

"You're so goddamn beautiful," he murmured, laying

me on the bed with infinite care. The moonlight streaming through the French doors painted silver shadows across his face as he looked down at me. "I've wanted this—wanted you—for so long."

"Show me," I breathed, pulling him down to me. "And let me show you how much I've been wanting you."

BANGASMCH

*S*ara Jayne was sparkling light and Christmas magic beneath me, her curves soft against my hands as I traced every beautiful inch of her. All those nights of holding back, pretending I didn't want to kiss the spot where her neck met her shoulder, or run my fingers along the delicate stretch marks on her hips, the sides of her breasts, and her belly that were thin silver ribbons in the darkness—they all led to this moment.

"I want you too much. Why did I ever think we should take it slow?" she whispered, pulling me down for a kiss that fritzed out every brain cell I had. Her hands mapped the muscles of my back while I explored the sweet curve of her waist, the full roundness of her breasts, perfect in my palms.

"All I want right now is to explore every part of you I've spent the past few weeks memorizing." I pressed kisses down her throat, loving how she arched into me.

"Every gorgeous inch." My lips found the swell of her breast. "Every perfect curve."

She shivered as my hands slid down to grip her hips, thumbs tracing those beautiful marks that told the story of her. Sara Jayne guided my hand between the plush swell of her thigh, guiding me to where she needed me the most. But since we'd waited this long, I was going to take my time lavishing attention on every spot from the top of her head to those delectable little toes.

"Let me, sweetheart." I murmured against her skin. "I've spent too long fantasizing this for you to hurry me past any single part of you."

She sucked in a soft breath. "You fantazize about me?"

"Oh, fuck yes, I do. Let me show you," I whispered, trailing kisses down the soft swell of her stomach. "Let me show you exactly what has me on Santa's naughty list this year."

I swirled my tongue around her belly button, wanting to give her a hint at exactly what I was dying to do. Her soft belly deserved to be worshipped just as much as the rest of her. Someday I hoped to feel our baby growing right here.

Her curves filled my hands as I worshipped my way down between her thighs and reveled in the sweet gasp and guttural sigh when I finally spread her legs, revealing a carefully sculpted thatch of hair and a delightfully bare pussy.

The glow of all the Christmas lights outside our window painted her skin in golden light and shadows, making her look like something out of a dream—except she was real, gloriously real, and finally mine.

"This right here has definitely earned me some coal in my stocking." The words fell between kisses and nips from the inside of one of her thighs to the other. I traced the curve of her inner thigh, licking my way up to the fullness of that plump pussy that was calling to me to revel in it. "Because I've definitely jacked off in the shower, imagining being right here, licking, and teasing, and tasting you, until you melt for me."

"Mac..." Her voice caught as my lips found that most sensitive spot, and I sucked her swollen clit between my teeth. "Please...yes. I need you, I need more."

I gave her exactly what she asked for and flicked my tongue over and over until her thighs were shaking and she was mumbling incomprehensibly... or actually, that might be German.

It was now my goal to get her to forget how to speak English because I fried her brain with my head between her legs. The way her moans were rising in pitch, she was close to coming, and I couldn't wait to push her over the edge.

"Mein gott." She slid one of her hands into my hair and gripped it tight. *"Oh, das fühlt sich so gut an. Genau da. Hör nicht auf."*

Later I was going to get her to teach me how to dirty talk in German too.

With one last move, I pushed two fingers inside her wet channel and that did it. She arched her back and her pussy clenched down hard on my fingers. *"Ja, ja, oh Gott, ja."*

My mind and body warred with whether I wanted to draw this orgasm out as long as I could, and crawling back up her body and finally getting to feel her pussy squeezing my cock like she was my fingers.

She made the decision for me, yanking me up to kiss me long and hard. I was absolutely loving how confident she was in her own sexuality, her body, and what she enjoyed. So many women I'd been with tried to hide themselves, wanted the lights out, or to leave some of their clothes on. Not my girl.

She fit herself against me, soft where I was hard, curves meeting angles like we were made for each other. When her legs wrapped around my hips, drawing me closer, the last threads of my control nearly snapped.

"Tell me what you want, sweetheart," I breathed against her lips. "Tell me you want me to fuck you."

"Mmm. I do want that, but it's my turn." She reached between our bodies and found my cock, giving it one hard stroke.

"If I knew how to swear in German, I would." I couldn't help but thrust into her hand even though I was far too turned on to let her touch me like this for very long. Not if I wanted to be inside of her tight pussy. And I very much wanted that. "But I promise, there are no turns. It makes me so fucking hot to see you come for me."

"Which I did." She swirled her fingers around my tip and my cock begged me to let her continue. "So now I want to make you come for me."

"Oh, honey. I promise I will." I grabbed her hand and pulled it back up, kissing her fingers. Then I grabbed a condom from the bedside table and pressed it into her hand. "But I want to come when I'm buried deep in your pretty pussy, and you're milking me with your third or fourth or fifth orgasm."

She waggled her eyebrows at me and slid the condom over my cock. "How did you know multiple orgasms are my favorite Christmas present?"

"Just because I'm on the naughty list doesn't mean you're not on the very, very good list."

"Ooh. Call me a naughty girl and give me orgasms, and I'll put you on my good list."

I barely gave her a chance to finish that sentence before I had her hands over her head and my cock at the entrance of her pussy. "We are both going to have so much fun exploring every single one of those kinks you've been hiding from me, naughty girl."

She wrapped her legs around my waist and I pushed just the tip of my cock in. Both of our eyes rolled back into our heads at the intensity of joining our bodies. But I took a deep breath and refocused on her. "Look at me, my sweet and sexy Sara Jayne. I want to see the swirls of lust in your eyes as I bury myself all the way into your wet pussy."

A few blinks and she looked up at me through her lashes. I was already lost in her. Lost in her eyes, her body, and I wanted nothing more than to get lost in her love.

"That's it." So slowly and torturously for us both, I thrust forward until I was filling her up.

She groaned and her eyes fluttered shut again."Oh, holy *Tannenbaum*."

I was taking that as a compliment. "You feel so fucking good. I'm afraid I'm going to embarrass myself and not be able to give you all those orgasms I promised before I lose my goddamn mind."

There was no way I was going to come before she did, but it was going to be a close thing. She was too beautiful, her body too perfectly fit to mine, and my feelings for her too intense to be in control.

Sara Jayne wrapped her ankles around my ass and arched her back into me. "Don't hold back. I want all of you. I'm giving myself to you, and I want only for you to do the same."

Best. Christmas present. Ever.

Not just that she wanted me, wanted me to fuck her, but that she was the first person in my life to want me for me. I was the dutiful son to my parents until they didn't need me anymore and flittered off to Florida. I was the all-star quarterback to my team until I was so injured I could never play again.

And I was the guy who made the deals and got the money for my clients, except there'd only ever been one client, and I wasn't sure I'd ever be the agent I wanted to be.

But Sara Jayne didn't want me for my skills, for what I could do for her. She wanted all of me, the good and the bad, the naughty and the nice.

"I'm yours, sweetheart. I'm yours." I move my hips and together we found a rhythm that had us both racing toward all the pleasure and bliss we could give each other. A few more thrusts and I was so damn close to coming. I needed to push her over the edge.

I squeezed her hands over her head tighter and buried my face into the crook of her neck, scraping my teeth across the soft skin of her neck. She moaned with each of my thrusts and her pussy tightened as her body tensed in anticipation of her climax. "That's it. Come for me, naughty girl."

"I need you to come with me."

This fucking woman was so damn perfect. I pressed my lips to her ear and whispered, my voice coming out broken and gravely. "Be a naughty girl and squeeze my cock hard. Make us both come with your hot pussy. Together."

Before I even finished telling her what to do, her whole body clenched and exploded around me. She dragged me so hard into that orgasm that I wasn't sure I would ever return. And I never wanted to.

The moment I could breathe again, could function, I rolled to the side, taking her with me so I didn't squish her under my weight. We were both gasping in shaky breaths, and I was seeing the damn northern lights behind my eyes.

Sara Jayne wrapped her arms around me and started shaking. At first I was worried the epicness of that orgasm had put her into shock, but she was giggling. "I don't know what that was, but it certainly wasn't boring couple sex."

I chuckled and stroked my hand through her hair, and she continued to lightly laugh against my chest. "Naughty girl sex is definitely not boring. You surprised me. I thought the kink was to be called a good girl."

She pulled her up and smiled up at me in a way that had me wanting to roll right back over and fuck her all over again.

"I've been the good girl my whole life. Always working hard, doing what I'm told, trying to be what everyone wants me to be. But today, with jumping into that photoshoot like that... it felt... naughty. And I liked it. I know it wasn't really, but I'm not sure that I would have had the... balls to do it a month, or even a couple of weeks ago."

"I don't believe that for a second. The moment I saw you trying to rescue a goose from the chopping block, I saw the deliciously naughty girl in you."

"I was just trying to save him from being eaten."

"Yeah, by chasing him through a busy beer tent, wrangling me along the way, and then turning him into a beloved media personality so he'd be safe for the rest of his life."

She shrugged and grinned. "I mean... somebody had to."

My delicious bad girl didn't even realize how she'd simply been growing into being the deliciously authentic version of herself. "Besides, only a naughty girl would fake an engagement to save me and her goose from being homeless."

"That was pretty naughty, wasn't it?" Her eyes sparkled, and she licked her lips.

And then the two of us were very naughty together all over again.

Sunlight streaming through the French doors woke me to the perfect sight of Sara Jayne curled against my chest, her hair a golden mess across my pillow. Last night felt like a dream, but the warm weight of her in my arms was beautifully real.

My phone buzzed on the nightstand. Then buzzed again. And again.

Sara Jayne stirred, mumbling something that sounded a lot like "turn off the goose," before snuggling closer.

I reached for the phone, trying not to disturb her. The notifications made me freeze.

Tommy Frayzer #HolidayProposal trending

Illustrated Sports drops behind-the-scenes footage of NFL star's surprise proposal

L.A. Bandits' running back engaged to plus-size model in viral Christmas shoot

"That's... not good," I muttered.

"Mmm?" Sara Jayne lifted her head, sleep-tousled and gorgeous. "What's not good?"

I showed her the screen just as an email notification popped up. This one was from a major athletic wear brand I'd been trying to get interested in doing a sponsorship with Tommy for months. They were one of the top reasons I was trying to get Tommy a better image.

I guess sexy Santa settling down with a naughty but nice girl was the image they wanted.

"Oh, no." She sat up, clutching the sheet to her chest. "The proposal shot. But it wasn't real."

"Try telling that to the internet." I scrolled through the comments on Illustrated Sports InstaSnap post. "Everyone loves Tommy, the bad boy with a heart of gold, proposing to the curvy model who helped reform his image."

"But we're the ones who are..." she trailed off, biting her lip.

"Actually in love?" I pulled her close, pressing a kiss to her temple. "Yeah, funny how that worked out."

Sara Janye's smile lit up the universe. "You're... you... did you?"

"Say I was in love with you?" I sure as shit did. And I meant it. "Because I am. I love you Sara Jayne."

She yanked me down for a soul deep kiss. *"Ich liebe Dich."*

I didn't need an interpreter for that one.

Her phone started ringing, and Magda's name flashed on the screen. Damn. We were in for... something. Magda thought Sara Jayne and I were engaged. She was going to either flip her lid or fire us from this house sitting job or, well, I had no idea. But we'd just gone from being the boring couple to something decidedly un-boring in the last twenty-four hours.

"Don't answer it," I said, but she was already reaching for it. I wanted to live in our little love bubble for just a smidgen longer.

"Magda, hi. I can explain—" She winced at whatever the woman who held her career in her hands was saying. "No, no, I'm not cheating on Mac, and I'm not engaged to Tommy. It was just part of the shoot. I'll get it cleared up..."

She glanced over at me with wide, worried eyes and shook her head. This wasn't going well. Shit. I had to do something to fix it. But what the hell that was, I had no idea.

Where was Sir Honksalot to the rescue with his particular brand of shattering any tension when you needed him?

"Yes, I know it's all over... What? How many booking inquiries?"

I watched her eyes go from worried to wide with surprise at whatever number Magda was saying. She grabbed my arm and squeezed. Something big was happening, and it didn't seem like it was anything bad.

Meanwhile, my own phone was blowing up with more inquiries of everything from a diamond ring company to pet food people suddenly very interested in Tommy's wholesome new image. I turned my phone for Sara Jayne to see and I didn't think her expressions could get anymore excited or surprised.

Sara Jayne hung up and we both just sat there stunned for a minute. "It's like the entire world wants me and Tommy. Just because we got fake engaged? I don't get it."

"Babe, it's not about the engagement... I don't think. It's the discoverability factor in being on the cover of Illustrated Sports. And..." this was going to kill me, but there was no way I was holding her back from a once in a lifetime opportunity to make her career, "I think you and Tommy shouldn't correct the media. Just go with it, and ride the wave of popularity while you can."

"What? No. I'm in love with you, remember?"

"Sweetheart. We both know that. I'm not going anywhere and my love isn't some fragile thing that a few rumors or misunderstandings can break by people out there in the world that don't matter. But this could be so good for your career, and honestly, Tommy's too. This could give us both the boost we need in our careers."

"Or it could blow up in our faces when everyone finds out it's not real."

She turned to face me, and even with this chaos brewing, all I could think about was how beautiful she looked wearing nothing but sunlight and my sheets. "That will not happen. You've already told Magda, and obviously Tommy knows. Those are the only people who could blow the secret. This will work."

It had to.

TINSEL AND TATAS

"Sir Honksalot, that wreath is not a snack!" Mac's voice came through my phone as I touched up my lipstick in the Crown of Curves reception area. "No—don't you give me that look. We talked about this."

An indignant honk, followed by a crash made me wince. "Everything okay there?"

"Oh sure. Our goose just thinks he's an interior decorator now. Apparently, the wreaths would look better on the floor. All of them."

I bit back a laugh. We'd only been officially together for a week, but hearing Mac say "our goose" still made my heart do funny things. "You knew what you were getting into when you agreed to goose-sit while Tommy was at practice and I was in Colorado."

"Yeah, well, next time you have a meeting with April de la Reine, you're taking the chaos machine with you."

"Somehow I don't think they want a goose at their brand launch meeting." I checked my reflection one last time. The emerald green wrap dress with the fur on the cuffs and hem hugged my curves perfectly, making me feel confident despite my nerves. "Though he does have more InstaSnap followers than their current spokes model."

"Speaking of social media..." Mac's voice turned cautious. "Have you seen the latest—"

The receptionist appeared. "Ms. Bauer? They're ready for you."

"Got to go. Love you. Don't let Sir Honksalot eat Santa." I would never tire of saying that. The love you part, not the eating Santa part. Unless, of course, Mac was dressed as sexy Santa when I got home.

"Too late for that warning," Mac sighed. "Love you too, *Liebling*."

Aww, he remembered the german pet name I'd called him at the airport. He was too cute for words.

I followed the receptionist down a hallway lined with gorgeous photos of plus-size models. My heart nearly stopped when I recognized April de la Reine's iconic lingerie campaign from five years ago—the one that had made me believe curves could be more than just "brave" or "controversial."

"Sara Jayne." April herself emerged from the conference room, absolutely glowing in a designer maternity dress. "I'm so glad you could make it. Thank you for flying out to Denver. I'm a bit too far along now and Bridger said no more flying. Oh, and congratulations on the engagement. I always knew that goose of yours would lead to romance."

Right. That. "About that—"

"Everyone's obsessed with IS's video and the cover of the magazine," she continued, ushering me into the room. "The spontaneity, the joy—it's exactly what we're looking for with Crown of Curves new line."

The conference room held several executives who all looked at me with that same excited recognition. Great.

"Now," April settled into her chair, one hand resting on her very pregnant belly that had seemed to have grown about a million times over since I saw her a month ago, "normally I'd be the face of our launch campaign, but baby Kingman number eight has other ideas. Which is actually perfect timing, because you're exactly what this brand needs."

"I am?"

"A fresh face in the plus-size world, already trending on this social media thing, America's new sweetheart thanks to that adorable photoshoot..." She grinned. "Not to mention you've got that natural confidence we want to showcase. Magda told me all about the way you handled that photoshoot disaster with the hockey player? Pure genius."

One of the executives—Janet, according to her nameplate—nodded enthusiastically. "We love how you're changing the conversation about plus-size modeling. No more 'brave' or 'controversial.' Just beautiful, confident, and so... authentically real."

"If we're lucky, because we're bidding late to get in, but we're shooting for a spot during the Bowl," April added. "Assuming the Bandits continue their winning streak, Tommy could be playing in that very game."

My stomach dropped. The Bowl. As in the championship of professional football? Where Tommy might be playing? Of course they would want that. Because everyone thought we were engaged.

"We're thinking a whole series," Janet continued. "Women from all walks of life, not just models. But we'd like to start with yours—the plus-size model who captured the heart of America's favorite bad-boy athlete."

April looked at Janet funny and then back at me, giving me a look that seemed to express she was sorry Janet was being so weird. "Maybe we can even include Sir Honksalot. The internet loves that goose."

My phone buzzed with a text from Mac.

> Update: Santa has been rescued, but the wreath is a lost cause. Also, you and Tommy are trending again. Something about #RelationshipGoals?

I looked around the table at all these people ready to believe in me, in what I could bring to their brand. Then down at Mac's text, proof of what was real in my life.

Sometimes the best opportunities come wrapped in complicated packages.

"So," April leaned forward, "what do you say? Ready to help us change the fashion world?"

I thought about all the girls like me who needed to see themselves as beautiful. About Mac, who loved me exactly as I was. About Sir Honksalot, who had somehow turned our chaos into something magical.

"I'm in," I said. "But you should know—"

A chorus of excited voices drowned out my attempt at honesty. As April began outlining their vision, my phone buzzed again.

> Don't worry about the trending stuff. We've got this. Also, Sir Honksalot says hi. At least I think that's what he meant. He might have just been asking for more treats.

I smiled. We did have this. Somehow.

Even if "this" now included a national fashion campaign built on a misunderstanding about my love life.

When the car from the airport dropped me back at the mansion, I found Mac on the front porch, watching Sir Honksalot arrange tinsel in the little evergreens on the steps with surprising artistic flair. Red and gold strands draped elegantly over the branches. There was also a brand new wreath hanging above the door.

"Is Sir Honksalot wearing the scarf and Santa hat from the photoshoot?"

"Your goose has opinions about holiday outfits and home decorating," Mac said, pulling me into his arms.

"Our goose," I corrected, loving how his chest rumbled with laughter. "And apparently he's developed a signature style."

"How was the meeting?"

"They want me as the face of their launch campaign." I snuggled closer, breathing in his familiar scent. "It's amazing, Mac. They're featuring women of all different careers and backgrounds who happen to be plus size. Athletes, executives, artists... showing that curves aren't something to overcome, they're just part of who these incredible women are."

"That's perfect for you." He pressed a kiss to my temple. "But I'm sensing a 'but' coming."

"The Bandits' PR lady called while I was at the airport waiting for my flight back." I pulled back to meet his eyes. "They want us—me and Tommy—to do some public appearances. Play up the 'romance' angle."

"Ah. Yeah, they called me too." His hands stayed warm on my waist. "And how do you feel about that?"

"Weird? I mean, everyone thinks I'm engaged to Tommy, but I'm actually in love with you, and it feels wrong to—"

"Help both our careers?" His smile was soft. "Sara Jayne, I know who you come home to. Who you love. If playing along with this misunderstanding for a while helps launch your modeling career and gets Tommy the sponsorship deals he deserves... I'm okay with that."

Sir Honksalot chose that moment to present us with a perfectly arranged piece of tinsel, looking ridiculously proud of himself.

"See?" Mac took the tinsel and draped it around my neck like a sparkly scarf. "Even our goose agrees. And he's very particular about his tinsel gifts."

"You're sure?" I wound my arms around his neck. "Because I don't want to do anything that might hurt us."

"The only thing that could hurt us would be passing up opportunities we've both worked so hard for." He kissed me softly. "Besides, Tommy's like my brother. If I have to pretend my girlfriend is engaged to anyone..."

"Your girlfriend, huh?"

His eyes darkened. "Well, I was thinking more like 'love of my life', but I didn't want to sound too cheesy."

"I like cheesy." I rose on tiptoes to kiss him properly, only to be interrupted by an indignant honk.

Sir Honksalot stood watching us, head tilted, another piece of tinsel held expectantly in his beak.

"I think," Mac laughed, "our goose is trying to tell us to focus on his artistic vision."

"Clearly, he gets his diva tendencies from Tommy."

"Speaking of Tommy..." Mac's phone buzzed. "The team wants us at the Christmas Day game. Owner's suite. It's kind of a big deal."

"Fancy." I accepted another piece of tinsel from our feathered decorator. "Think they'll let us bring Sir Honksalot?"

"Let's not push our luck." Mac watched as our goose waddled back to his bushes, clearly planning his next masterpiece. "Though I have a feeling the suite could use his decorating expertise. Christmas at the game isn't exactly festive."

I leaned into him, watching Sir Honksalot work. Sometimes the best plans are the ones you never meant to make. And sometimes the best love stories start with a little chaos.

Even if that chaos currently involved explaining to our goose why he couldn't wear the Christmas tree star as a hat.

The owner's suite at Bandits Stadium was about as rich and luxurious as I'd expected. Although, Mac was right and there was only the bare minimum of holiday decorations. A wreath on the door and some twinkle lights. Boring. Mac squeezed my hand as Violet Wolfner, the Bandits' owner, waved us over.

"The dynamic duo ala Tommy Frayzer." She air-kissed my cheeks. "I have to tell you, that Illustrated Sports shoot was genius. Tommy's Q score is through the roof."

Through the floor-to-ceiling windows, I could see the Bandits warming up on the field. Tommy was easy to spot, playing to the crowd as always. The Denver Mustangs' defense looked considerably less festive about the whole thing.

"Mac," Violet turned to him, "the way you've handled Tommy's image transformation is impressive. From karaoke disaster to America's sweetheart in two months? That takes skill."

"Sara Jayne deserves the credit," Mac said, his hand warm on my lower back. "She's the one who understood how to make Tommy relatable."

"By using a goose as a social media influencer?" Violet laughed. "Speaking of which, my granddaughter insisted we put one of those decorator geese on our porch. Apparently it's the must-have holiday accessory this year. Who knew?"

I bit back a smile, thinking of Sir Honksalot in his heated doghouse, probably reorganizing his tinsel collection. If they only knew he'd accidentally started L.A.'s hottest holiday decorating trend. Every house on Magda's block had a porch goose, and it appeared to have spread from there. Maybe they'd keep them out after the holidays and dress them up for all the seasons? Or would that be weird? I kind of liked the idea. We should send one to Mac's parents after the new year for their new house.

"Now then," Violet gestured to the catering spread, "help yourselves. And Mac? During a lull in the game, I'd like to discuss representation for some of our other players. They've got some shit agents, and I've encouraged a few of them to talk to you."

Mac's eyes widened slightly. This was huge—the opportunity he'd been working toward for years. "Yes, ma'am. That would be great."

She nodded and turned back to me, taking my arm in hers and walking us both toward the buffet. "Now, I'd like to know just who dresses you. I have the hardest time finding anything in a size sixteen or eighteen in L.A. and I refuse to kowtow to the diet industry and culture. Heroine chic might be chronic, but my ass is iconic."

Oh, I think Crown of Curves was about to get a new fan, and maybe a tagline.

The game itself was a blur of excitement. Tommy played like a man possessed, breaking through the Mustangs' defense like they were standing still. When he scored the winning touchdown with seconds left on the clock, the suite erupted in cheers.

I screamed and wrapped Mac in an enormous hug, but then jumped back, catching myself from doing more and giving him a big kiss. "That's our Tommy!"

Violet's knowing look made me wonder if she saw more than she let on.

Later we all went out to Club Midnight, where they were having an all night long Christmas celebration. While I was on Tommy's arm, I watched Mac chatting with some players who'd approached him about representation. He caught my eye across the room and smiled that smile that still made my knees weak.

"You two are terrible at hiding it, you know," Tommy said, handing me a glass of champagne with little bobbing Santa candies floating around in the bubbles.

"Hiding what?"

"The fact that you're stupid in love with each other." He clinked his glass against mine. "Don't worry, though. The rest of the world is having too much fun with our 'romance' to notice."

He grinned. "Speaking of which, want to dance with your fake fiancé? Give the paparazzi outside something to talk about?"

I laughed, letting him pull me onto the dance floor. "You're enjoying this way too much."

"Hey, my best friend is finally happy. I'm playing the best football of my career, and there's a decorative goose wearing my jersey number on Violet Bidwill Wolfner's front porch. Life is good."

It was. Just as long as nobody found out all of our not so little secrets.

I found Mac in a quiet corner in the VIP section, his expression adorably confused as he scrolled through his phone.

"Hey you," I said, sliding next to him. "Everything okay?"

"I think I might have a problem." He showed me his phone. "Three different players just asked me about getting them a goose. I mean, Sir Honksalot is one of a kind, and I'm not sure I'm equipped to handle an entire roster of clients with waterfowl. The fountain budget alone would be—"

I burst out laughing, drawing curious looks from nearby partygoers. "Mac, *Liebling*, they're talking about porch geese. The decorative ones?"

"The what now?"

"It's the new holiday trend. Everyone in L.A. has them. Fake geese wearing seasonal outfits?" I bit my lip to keep from giggling at his bewildered expression. "You seriously haven't noticed that every house in our neighborhood has one?"

"I thought they were just really into Sir Honksalot."

"Well, technically they are." I curled into him, lowering my voice. "Our goose apparently started a movement. I showed him my phone, where #PorchGoose was trending alongside photos of increasingly elaborate goose displays. "Want to tell Sir Honksalot he's a style icon?"

"Absolutely not. He's impossible enough about his tinsel arrangement as it is."

Mac's laugh rumbled through his chest. He glanced around quickly, and seeing no one paying attention, pulled me deeper into the alcove. "Have I told you lately how much I love you?"

"Mmm, not in the last hour."

His kiss was soft, sweet, and over far too quickly. But the way he looked at me after—like I was everything he'd ever wanted—made my heart go flippity floppy.

"I love how you thought you needed to source emotional support geese for professional athletes."

Another quick kiss, this one with a promise of more

later. "I love how you make everything in my life better, even the chaos."

We rejoined the party, maintaining our careful distance, but I caught Mac watching me throughout the night with that soft expression that made me forget about fake engagements and viral trends. This—us—was real. Everything else was just decoration.

THE BIG BOWL

"Sir Honksalot, the TV camera crew does not need your creative input." I adjusted my tie while watching our goose attempt to direct the Espy TV team breaking down after their coverage this morning in the living room side our luxury suite at the swanky, brand new Five Elements hotel Denver. Apparently having America's favorite "engaged" couple and their viral sensation goose warranted pre-game coverage.

The fact that they were filming the wrong couple was a detail I tried not to dwell on.

"He's just excited." Sara Jayne appeared in our bedroom doorway, taking my breath away in a vintage-inspired Bandits jersey dress that hugged every perfect curve. She'd gotten ready in Tommy's adjoining room so as not to raise suspicion with the TV crew. "Though I think he's more interested in the cameraman's shoelaces than his cinematography."

"You look amazing." I checked quickly to make sure no one was paying attention to us, and pulled her close, breathing in her familiar vanilla scent. The week in Denver had been surreal—joint interviews, press conferences, and trying to keep Sir Honksalot from redecorating the hotel's lobby. "Almost makes me wish we could skip all this and stay here."

"On the big Bowl Sunday? When your client is favored to take the MVP title?" She straightened my tie. "Besides, you have meetings with three potential new clients today."

"Four, actually. Turns out helping Tommy reform his image is good for business." I caught her hand, pressing a kiss to her palm. "You okay with all this? The cameras, the pressure..."

"Are you?" Her eyes searched mine. "It's not exactly easy watching your girlfriend play happy couple with your best friend."

"Hey." I tucked a strand of hair behind her ear. "I know who you love. The rest is just... strategic career advancement."

She laughed. "Very romantic."

"I'll show you romantic later." I leaned in for a kiss, only to be interrupted by an indignant honk.

Sir Honksalot stood in the doorway, wearing what appeared to be a miniature referee jersey. I didn't want to know where he'd gotten it.

"Tommy's been shopping again," Sara Jayne said and laughed. "He's got a Bandit's jersey for later when this silly goose is slated to join The Boys for their pre-game show. I'm thinking we should hire a full-time animal wrangler like we've had this week at home."

"Have to make sure our good luck charm was properly dressed," Tommy called from the adjoining doorway, adjusting his own game day suit. "You see the feature they did on him yesterday? 'From Delinquent Duck to big Bowl Sensation.'"

The suite's phone rang, and the concierge let us know our car service to the stadium was here, as was the team's bus to the stadium. Time to become the power agent with the hottest client in the League and his supermodel fiancée. Even if that fiancée actually belonged to me.

The scene outside was chaos. The players all boarded their bus for the stadium. Cameras flashed as we emerged together, the perfect picture of a star player, his supportive fiancée, and their social media famous goose. I slipped into agent mode, fielding questions about Tommy's preparation, his incredible season, the transformation of his public image.

The gauntlet to the stadium was fraught with paparazzi. Good thing Sara Jayne was a model and knew exactly how to handle them. I did not love having my picture taken near as much. I was grateful when we got to the ticket holders' only area and walked past the windows on the way to the owner's suite.

On the field, Tommy was putting on a show during warmups. The Denver crowd might have come to boo the Bandits, but they couldn't help cheering when he caught a behind-the-back pass while doing the Macarena.

When we arrived, a familiar voice called out. Coach Bridger Kingman stood near the entrance with April and a few of their kids. "Mac, good to see you again. I'd like to introduce you to my two eldest, this is Chris, and Declan. They may be in need of your services someday."

That surprised the shit out of me. Their grandfather

was Hunter De la Reine who owned one of the oldest and most prestigious agency in... the world.

Twelve-year-old Chris was practically vibrating with excitement, while his brother Declan seemed more interested in the buffet. A tiny baby slept peacefully in a contraption strapped to April's chest, somehow immune to the noise.

"That game-winning drive at Oregon, where you threw that pass with a broken arm, and a torn ACL," Chris said, eyes shining. "Dad shows it to his quarterbacks all the time when they're being whiners."

I tried not to wince at the mention of my football career's end point. "Your dad's got a few legendary plays of his own to show them too, I'm sure."

"Mac, darling." Violet Wolfner said, appearing beside us. The Bandits' owner looked elegant, as always in her trademark purple suit. "I see you're already acquainted with The Kingmans. I just had to have the championship coach of my alma mater here with me today, didn't I?"

Coach Kingman gave a nod in deference. "Winning has its perks."

"Along with several other guests who I've already heard are very interested in your work with Tommy." Her knowing look made me wonder if she saw more than she let on. "Sometimes the best stories are the ones we don't expect. The ones that surprise us."

I didn't know what that meant, and I didn't get to ask because the game started and April and Sara Jayne waved me and Coach Kingman over to sit with them.

The owner's suite was a study in controlled chaos during the game, but at halftime, it doubled. The animal wrangler brought Sir Honksalot up who had immediately charmed Declan and Chris, who were now teaching him plays—or trying to. April rocked her baby girl while sharing knowing looks with Sara Jayne that made me nervous. And Violet Wolfner had me cornered with three different team owners who all wanted to know how I'd engineered Tommy's remarkable image transformation.

"It's all about authenticity," I explained, trying not to get distracted by how beautiful Sara Jayne looked laughing with April, especially when she took the baby and cooed at her. "Tommy's always had heart. We just helped people see it."

"Speaking of heart," one of the owners said, nodding toward where Sara Jayne was now holding baby Jules, "that engagement story is pure gold. The bad boy reformed by love—and a rescue goose."

"And those viral videos," another added. "The goose doing touchdown dances? Brilliant marketing."

Sir Honksalot chose that moment to demonstrate his own touchdown dance, sending the Kingman boys into fits of laughter.

"Mac?" Bridger Kingman pulled me aside as the owners moved on. "Chris has been talking about you non-stop since he found out you'd be here. Says you're exactly the kind of agent he wants when he goes pro."

My heart skipped a beat and then trampolined on my stomach. Chris Kingman was already being called the next great quarterback prospect, and he was only twelve. "That's... wow. I mean, he's got years before he needs an agent, and I thought he'd go with the De la Reines."

"Just something to think about. April wants the boys to

make their own decision about who they want to represent them. She's big on them earning their way in the world and not resting on their laurels or family wealth or influence." Bridger's eyes crinkled. "It's important to her to raise good men."

"From what I can see, you two are doing a great job." I wished everyone had parents like they did. Maybe they wouldn't end up hanging out with strippers and singing karaoke sockless if they had.

The first half of the bowl had been a defensive battle, but in the second, Tommy caught fire. Two touchdown receptions, one running score, and a trick play that had the announcers screaming. By the fourth quarter, the Bandits were up 21-7 and it was sure looking like the Tigers were going down.

Sara Jayne was talking with one of the owners and there was something in the way she was holding herself that said she was not enjoying that conversation. I made a beeline for her and stepped right in between her and the man making her feel uncomfortable.

"Hey, Sara Jayne," I didn't even acknowledge the suit. "I just got a call about that thing. Can you approve it for me right now?"

"Sure. Yeah. Of course." She nodded to the owner and took a few steps toward the door.

"I need some air," Sara Jayne whispered and jerked her chin toward the suite's door. No one noticed us slip out—except maybe April, who suddenly became very interested in showing Sir Honksalot's outfit to the baby.

The service corridor was quiet, empty. Sara Jayne's hands shook slightly as she leaned against the wall.

"Hey." I stepped closer, unable to resist touching her. "You okay? Did that douchecanoe say something to you? I will kick his ass and call him out on shit behavior even if he is the owner of the Miami Hammerheads."

"No, no. He was just asking all these questions about me and Tommy. Like he didn't think it was real. It was just... a lot of lies and pretending." She looked up at me with those eyes that had owned me since Oktoberfest. "Sometimes I just want to tell everyone the truth. That I'm in love with you, not Tommy. That this whole thing is—"

I cut her off with a kiss. Couldn't help it. She melted into me, her hands sliding into my hair as mine found her waist. For a perfect moment, there was no pretense, no complications. Just us.

There was someone else further down the hallway, but I couldn't tell, and honestly didn't care at this point, how far away they were.

"We should get back," Sara Jayne murmured against my lips.

"Two more minutes," I breathed, pulling her closer. We both needed this little breather, but when the stadium erupted into cheers and boos, it was time to rejoin the world. The world that didn't include me and Sara Jayne and a happy ever after.

After today, I wanted what the Kingmans had. A beautiful and strong wife, a family of amazing kids, and love. So much love.

As soon as I could figure out how, I was ending this charade. Tommy and Sara Jayne were both at the top of their games right now. It wouldn't hurt either of them if they "broke up". Especially not after the conversation I'd had with the owner of the Miami Hammerheads. They wanted Tommy, who was a free-agent after this season.

Sure, the Bandits would want him back too, but I wasn't sure Violet would be willing to pony up the money the Sharks were prepared to offer. So Sara Jayne and Tommy could break it off because they didn't want to do the long distance relationship thing. That was totally plausible.

"You go back in first. I'll follow. Just gonna make a quick phone call first." I gave Sara Jayne a gentle push toward the suite. "Go cheer Tommy on."

I watched her walk back into the suite and sent off a quick email to the Miami owner's secretary confirming that he wanted me to get on their president's calendar. A couple of giggling women wearing Tiger's jerseys, probably other players' WAGs walked past, and then I headed back in to watch the rest of the game, knowing that I was going to make my future everything I wanted it to be.

The fourth quarter was pure magic. Tommy seemed to be playing in a different dimension, breaking tackles, finding impossible routes. When he caught the game-winning touchdown with thirteen seconds left, the stadium erupted.

"MVP! MVP!" The chant started in our suite and spread through the stands like wildfire.

Sir Honksalot added his own triumphant honk to the championship atmosphere. Even baby Jules woke up to join the celebration, gurgling happily in April's arms.

My phone buzzed. Probably another potential client. I'd already made appointments with two defensive tackles from the Mustangs during the game—

The text wasn't from a client.

> Check ZMT. Now.

Then another.

> What the hell, Mac?

And another.

> OMG did Tommy's fiancée cheat with his agent???

Then,

> Oops, wrong person.

My stomach dropped as I opened the link on the first text. There we were, Sara Jayne and I, wrapped around each other in that quiet hallway moments ago. The photos were grainy but unmistakable. The headlines were worse:

SUPER BOWL SCANDAL: Tommy Frayzer's Fiancée Caught with His Agent in a Love Triangle that Rocks the League's Biggest Day. Cinderella Story Turns Toxic.

Across the suite, Sara Jayne's phone was lighting up too. I watched the color drain from her face as she read. Even Sir Honksalot seemed to sense something was wrong, abandoning his game of catch with the Kingman boys to waddle to her side.

"Mac?" Violet appeared at my elbow. "We need to get ahead of this. Now."

"I'll handle it," I started, but she cut me off.

"You're trending almost as much as Tommy's MVP performance. This could destroy everything we've built."

Tommy. Oh god. He was down there celebrating the biggest moment of his career, and I'd just turned it into a tabloid scandal.

"Sara Jayne?" April's voice carried over the chaos. She'd handed Jules to Bridger and was now steering Sara Jayne toward a private corner, dragon-mama mode fully activated.

"I've got PR on standby," Violet said. "But they need to know what statement to make. Was this a onetime thing? Tell me you were just trying to get an eyelash off her face or something stupid. What's the story we're selling?"

The truth stuck in my throat. Any version would hurt someone. No matter what we said either we were going to destroy Magda's faith in Sara Jayne, ruin her reputation, and probably her career. And even if we denied everything, it was going to tank Tommy's big moment and probably my agency's future. No one was going to want to sign on with a cheater or a liar.

"Mac." Sara Jayne's voice was steady despite her pale face. She crossed to me, Sir Honksalot trailing protectively behind her. "What are we going to tell them? No one is going to believe the truth now."

"What truth?" Violet demanded.

I looked at Sara Jayne—really looked at her. The woman who'd jumped to save a dead-man-walking goose. Who'd turned chaos into magic. Who'd made every part of my life better just by being in it.

"The truth," I said, taking her hand. "All of it. It's the only way."

From the field below, the MVP chants grew louder. But soon enough, someone would show Tommy these pictures and ask him how he felt. It wasn't like he was going to be hurt. He'd been rooting for us all along. But even he would understand the repercussions of this lie getting out.

We just had to figure out how to tell it without breaking everything we'd built.

FAKING IT WAS NOT MAKING IT

"In here," Tommy yanked us into what appeared to be a storage room, shutting out the chaos of reporters shouting questions about betrayal and scandal. His jersey was still damp with champagne and sweat, his eyes wild with the same adrenaline that had won them the game.

"Tommy, I'm so sorry, we didn't mean—" I started, but he waved me off.

"Are you kidding? This is the most excitement we've had since Sir Honksalot crashed that Oktoberfest tent." Wait. I thought he was passed out for that.

He peered out the small window. "Though the press corps are getting creative with their theories. Apparently, according to those yahoos, I've known about your affair for weeks and I've been drowning my sorrows in karaoke again."

"This isn't funny," Mac said, his hand warm on my lower back. "They're overshadowing your MVP moment. Everything you've worked for—"

"Okay, options." Tommy cut Mac off and started pacing. "We could say Sara Jayne and I already broke up because I'm leaving L.A."

"What?" I looked at Mac, who suddenly found the floor fascinating.

"Miami's interested," he admitted. "Big money. Fresh start. We've been in talks, but..."

"But they're super hush, hush. Violet doesn't know yet," Tommy finished. "And if this gets out before the deal's done..."

"It's dead." Mac ran a hand through his hair. "Along with any chance of other teams offering either. Violet will know she can keep you for a song. Not to mention all the prospective clients I've got coming in ghosting me. They probably are already planning too anyway at this point."

I knew what that felt like. Magda had been texting me constantly for the last hour with cancelled gigs. At least April and Crown of Curves weren't giving up on me yet.

The weight of everything we could lose pressed against my chest. My entire career was about to be back to pre-Illustrated Sports days. Mac's growing agency was shrinking by the second. Tommy's carefully rebuilt image was possibly trashed.

All because people loved to gossip and loved a fall from grace even more.

"I could just tell them the truth." Tommy stopped pacing. "That this was all fake because I'm—"

"No." Mac said. "I wish you could, Tom. I wish the league, the public, the world was ready. But it means the end of your career and you know it."

I looked between the two of them. "Because you're what?"

Tommy gave me one of those fake slugs on the arm. "Because I'm gay, babe. If I come out, no one will question that we were never together and that you being with Mac is fine by me."

Oh. "But it's the twenty-first century. It's not like being gay is illegal."

Tommy shrugged and Mac shook his head."Unfortunately, there's a lot of bigoted people in sports. Honestly, in America. People who can't see past their distorted values enough to understand that gay men are actual people... with feelings. The League isn't ready. The sponsors aren't ready. Tommy's career would be over if he came out. No one has ever been openly gay in the League. And even at the top of his game, MV Fucking P of the Bowl, today is not the day they'll all suddenly be okay with it."

Tommy clenched his fists and his expression went dark and angry. Something I'd never seen on him before. "Maybe it's time someone changed that."

"Not like this." Mac's voice was fierce. "Not because you're trying to save us. We won't let you sacrifice everything you've worked for."

I took one of Tommy's huge hands in mine. "I appreciate you trust me enough to share your true authentic self with me. And I want you to know that you're always safe with me. But Tommy, I don't want you to put your livelihood or even your actual safety in jeopardy."

A sharp knock made us all jump.

"Frayzer!" a harried PR rep called through the door. "Press room. Now. Unless you want a riot on your hands."

Tommy's face shifted, that familiar mischievous glint returning to his eyes. "Actually, I know exactly what to do."

"Tommy..." Mac's warning tone made me nervous.

"Trust me." He straightened his jersey. "Nobody's losing anything today. Well, except maybe their dignity when they realize how wrong they got this entire story."

"What are you going to say?" I asked, worried. I knew what it was like to be shamed and chastised just for being who I was.

He just grinned and opened the door. "The truth. Sort of. A better version of it."

"Tommy!"

But he was already gone, leaving us staring at each other in the sudden quiet.

"Should we be worried?" I asked Mac.

"With Tommy? Always."

Another knock, more insistent. "Mr. Frayzer's fiancée? Comment on the photos?"

I slammed the door on the jackass misogynistic reporter.

Mac pulled me close. "I don't know what the hell Tommy is about to do, but whatever happens, we face it together."

"Together," I agreed, and somehow it felt like a bigger promise than our fake engagement ever was.

Now we just had to hope Tommy's "better version" of the truth didn't make everything worse.

The press room was a mob scene. From our spot in the

back, Mac and I watched Tommy take the podium, still in his grass-stained jersey, the MVP trophy gleaming beside him. Camera flashes erupted like lightning.

"Mr. Frayzer! Comment on the photos—"

"Is it true that your fiancée—"

"How long has the affair—"

Tommy held up a hand, and somehow that cocky grin of his silenced the room. "First, let me say something about being MVP—"

"What about the photos of your fiancée with your agent?"

"Actually," Tommy's grin widened, "that's a funny story. See, Sara Jayne's not my type."

The room erupted again. Mac's hand found mine in the chaos.

"And more importantly," Tommy continued, "she's exactly Mac's type. Has been since the day he chased a goose through a beer tent at Oktoberfest for her."

My heart stopped. Started. Stopped again.

"What are you saying?" someone called out.

"I'm saying my best friend and agent is an idiot who wouldn't know how to tell a girl he's in love with her if his life depended on it. So yeah, I might have orchestrated a little something to push him in the right direction."

Murmurs rippled through the crowd. I felt Mac tense beside me.

"You're claiming the engagement was fake?"

"I'm claiming," Tommy leaned into the mic, "that you all need to pay better attention. Show me one photo—just one—of me and Sara Jayne together without Mac. Go ahead, I'll wait."

The furious tapping of phones filled the room.

"While you're searching," Tommy continued, "let me tell you about my best friend. The guy who, when he knew his own chances of getting into the League were over, became an agent to help the rest of us fulfill that dream. Who believed in me when I was nothing but a karaoke disaster with a bad reputation. Who fell in love with a girl and her rescue goose but was too scared to admit it."

"But the proposal video—" someone started.

"Was me being a supportive friend. Which, by the way, is what you should all be focused on right now. Did you see that game-winning drive? That's the actual story here. That, and the fact that sometimes it takes a village—or in this case, a very smart goose—to get two people to admit what everyone else already knows."

The room had gone quiet, phones forgotten.

"So yeah," Tommy's voice softened, "those photos you're all worked up about? That's what love actually looks like. And if you're done trying to manufacture scandal, I'd like to talk about how my team just won the mother fucking championship."

Mac's arm slid around my waist, pulling me closer. I looked up to find him watching me with that expression that still made my knees weak.

"Did he just..." I whispered.

"Save our careers by telling the truth in the most Tommy way possible?" Mac's smile was soft. "Yeah, I think he did."

From the podium, Tommy caught our eye and winked.

"Now, who wants to talk about that amazeballs fourth quarter drive..."

The press corps erupted with football questions, scandal forgotten. In the back of the room, I turned into Mac's arms, not caring who saw.

Sometimes the best love stories are the ones you don't have to fake at all.

The so-called scandal was so forgotten, that by the time we got to the after party, no one even looked twice at us.

"Have you seen this one?" Mac held up his phone, showing a blurry photo from Oktoberfest. "Someone caught the exact moment I jumped the keg of beer to help you catch Sir Honksalot."

We were curled up in a quiet-ish corner of the party, watching the internet absolutely lose it over Tommy's press conference. #RealLoveStory and #GooseMatchmaker were trending, along with some creative edits of Sir Honksalot wearing a tiny Cupid outfit.

"Oh my god," I laughed, taking the phone. "Look at your face! You're already completely gone for me."

"Obviously." He pressed a kiss to my temple. "Though not as gone as Tommy looks in this one."

The next photo showed Tommy at that same Oktoberfest, clearly playing matchmaker as he "accidentally" pushed Mac toward me. The caption read: *The real MVP: Tommy Frayzer's two-year plan to get his best friend the girl.*

"Two years?" I raised an eyebrow. "We met three months ago."

"Yeah, but it makes a better story this way. And you can't expect the press to get all the deets right, can you?"

Tommy dropped into the chair across from us, MVP trophy tucked under one arm. "The internet has decided I'm some kind of romantic genius who's been plotting this since I signed with you."

"Speaking of plotting..." Mac started.

"That was amazing," I cut in, reaching for Tommy's hand. "What you did in there. How you turned it around. Thank you."

"Please." Tommy grinned. "I just told the truth. With some creative timeline adjustment."

My phone buzzed. "Magda says Sir Honksalot is getting interview requests. Apparently, he's being called 'The Goose Who Started It All.'"

"Well, he did." Tommy stretched, looking satisfied. "Face it—none of us would be here if he hadn't decided to go rogue at Oktoberfest."

Mac's arm tightened around me. "Best wild goose chase ever."

The party swirled around us—players celebrating, media praising Tommy's MVP performance, social media exploding with our unexpected love story. But in our quiet corner, it felt like everything had finally fallen into a perfect, chaotic place.

"You know," Tommy said, a familiar glint in his eye, "Sir Honksalot's going to need a formal outfit for the wedding."

"The what now?" Mac choked on his champagne.

"Hey, according to the internet, you two have been secretly in love for years. Might want to catch up to your own love story."

Mac took my hand in his and rubbed his fingers over

the spot on my fourth finger where a ring would be. "I think it's time we call it a night, don't you, *Liebling*?"

The Five Elements lobby was mercifully quiet when we finally made it back from the party. Even Sir Honksalot seemed ready to wind down, his Bandit's jersey slightly askew from all the victory celebrations.

"Come on, chaos machine," Mac said fondly, scooping up our goose and taking him to Tommy's room. "Time for bed."

In the suite, Sir Honksalot waddled straight to his heated bed by the window, arranged his collection of "borrowed" socks from Tommy into a perfect nest, and settled in with a contented honk.

"I think the excitement finally got to him," I said, watching our feathered matchmaker drift off to sleep.

"Can't blame him." Mac pulled me into his arms. "It's been a big day. Winning the Bowl, saving our careers, becoming a social media romantic icon..."

"Speaking of..." I showed him my phone, where #GooseLoveStory was still trending. "Apparently we're now the greatest romance since *"The Princess Bride"*. Though I'm pretty sure that movie didn't involve any waterfowl."

"Their loss." His hands slid down to my hips, drawing me closer. "You know what the best part about all this is?"

"Hmm?"

"I get to do this whenever I want now." He kissed me softly, then with growing heat. "No more hiding. No more pretending."

"Just us," I breathed against his lips. "Being real."

His hands traced my curves with reverent familiarity,

like he was memorizing me all over again. "Do you know how many times I wanted to kiss you like this in public? Show everyone that you're mine?"

"Show me now," I whispered, and his kiss deepened, filled with all the love we'd been hiding.

He walked me backward toward our bed, his touch setting fire to every inch of skin he found. When my legs hit the mattress, he followed me down, his weight deliciously solid against me.

"I love you," he murmured, trailing kisses down my neck. "The genuine kind. The forever kind."

"Show me that too." I wriggled underneath Mac, loving the feel of his body covering mine. But something was poking me right in the left side of my belly. It wasn't the Christmas tree in Mac's pants either. This was too small for that.

"Mr. Jerry, is that a goose egg in you pocket or are you just happy to see me?"

Mac chuckled and slid off the end of the bed and onto one knee. He pulled a little black box out of his pocket. "It's not a goose egg, Sara Jayne."

SAY YES TO THE CHAOS

My grandmother's ring felt like it was burning a hole in my pocket, just like it had every day since I'd picked it up from the safe deposit box three weeks ago. But this time, as I dropped to one knee beside our hotel bed, everything felt different. Real.

Sara Jayne's eyes went wide. "Mac..."

"Remember when Magda asked why you weren't wearing a ring at her party?" My voice was steadier than I'd expected, probably because I'd never been more sure of anything in my life. "And I said I was waiting to get my grandmother's ring?"

She nodded, one hand pressed to her lips.

"That wasn't entirely a lie." I opened the box, revealing the vintage diamond that had been in my family for three generations. "I really did get it. That day. Because even though we were pretending, I knew—I think I've known since you ran through the tent chasing a goose at Oktoberfest—that you were it for me. Though I think the goose chased me, technically."

"Mac," she whispered again, tears sparkling in her eyes.

"I love how you color-code your sock drawer but will jump into chaos to help a friend. I love that you saw past my spreadsheets and planning, trying to figure out how to be successful, to the guy who needed a little chaos in his life. I love that you turned our fake engagement into the realest thing I've ever known." I took a shaky breath. "Sara Jayne, will you marry me? Hint, this is a real proposal this time."

A loud honk startled us both. Sir Honksalot stood in the doorway between the suites, watching us with what could only be described as an expectant expression.

Sara Jayne laughed through her tears. "I think our goose is waiting for an answer."

"Our goose isn't the only one."

"Yes," she said, pulling me up to her. "Yes to marrying you. Yes to chaos and color-coding and everything in between. Yes to our silly goose and our crazy life and—"

I cut her off with a kiss, sliding the ring onto her finger where it belonged. Where it had always belonged, even when we were just pretending.

Sir Honksalot let out another approving honk before settling back into his nest of stolen socks, apparently satisfied with his matchmaking work.

"I love you," I murmured against Sara Jayne's lips. "The genuine kind. The forever kind."

The moonlight caught the diamond on her finger as she pulled me onto the bed with her. My grandmother's ring—now her ring—sparkled just like her eyes.

"I can't believe you had this all along," she whispered, wrapping her arms around my neck.

"I can't believe you said yes." Actually I could. We belonged together, her and me, and we both knew it. I traced the curve of her cheek. "Sir Honksalot didn't really give you much choice."

Her laugh turned into a soft gasp as I found that sensitive spot below her ear and dragged my teeth across it just as she liked. "As if I'd ever say no to you."

My hands slid down her sides, exploring every perfect curve as if this was our first time together all over again. I needed her bare so I could worship her body in the way which she deserved. As my curvy, gorgeous goddess. Her dress joined my jacket on the floor. I traced kisses down her neck, pausing at the lace edge of her bra. "Is this new?"

"Mmm hmm. Crown of Curves new intimates collection. I got a free preview to test out."

"Remind me to send them a thank you note."

She laughed, the sound turning into a gasp as my hands found bare skin. "I don't think it's standard business practice to thank a clothing company for turning you on."

She melted into my touch as I pulled the cups of the pretty lace bra down to expose her nipples. In no time I licked my way from one to the other and back again. Every soft inch of her was perfect and delicious and most importantly, mine. Finally, truly mine.

"You're wearing too many clothes," she murmured, making quick work of my shirt buttons. Her hands slid down my chest. "To a very hot former quarterback. Did I mention I saw some of your game footage today?"

"I've still got game, sweetheart." I caught her hands, pressing kisses to her fingers, lingering on the ring.

"I'm a fan of your game," she breathed, pulling me closer, wrapping her legs around my hips. "But I have a few moves of my own."

I don't know how she did it, but she used her position to flip me right the hell over, so she was on top of me. "See? Now I'm having my way with you and there's nothing you can do about it."

Like I'd want to.

"Have your way... away." I waved my hands and perhaps gave my hips a good wiggle, letting the tent in my pants hit her in just the right spot.

"Oh my god, no fair, I'm supposed to be making your eyes roll back in your head, not the other way around." She moved her hips back and forth, sliding across my zipper covered erection.

"Trust me, baby. You're doing something to my head all right." I could do nothing but watch as she cupped her breasts and continued to thrust against me. No, that wasn't true. There was something I could do. I grabbed her hips and helped her move over me, my dick getting harder and harder for her. "Fuck, Sara Jayne, you're going to make me come in my pants if you keep up this lap dance."

She slowed and smiled down at me in a way that had me falling in love with her all over again. I'd let her dry hump me to completion if she wanted to. I was fucking mesmerized by her.

"I'd rather you were coming inside of me."

Okay, that was it. I flipped Sara Jayne back over and

dropped my pants and boxers faster than a speeding bullet. She giggled as I pulled her lace panties down her legs right after that, but had the foresight to finally slip out of her bra so we were both gloriously naked.

I crawled up the bed, kissing my way from her knees, up to her thighs, gave her pussy one quick French kiss, but continued on to her breasts, and then finally those soft, pink lips. "I'd rather come inside of you, too. And someday, if it's what you want to, I'd like to put a baby in your belly, and make even more of a family with you than we have now."

I'd been smart enough to grab a condom from my pants before getting back on the bed with her. "But for tonight, put this on me, and let me make you come so hard you don't just forget how to speak English, you forget your own name."

"You like it when I put the condom on you?" She opened the little packet and rolled the sheath down my cock.

When it was on, I thrust into her hands. "Yes, because it's the best way I know of to make sure you feel safe."

"I always am when I'm with you."

God, I loved her so much. I twisted us again, because it was clear my girl wanted to try being on top. I gripped her lush thighs and spread them so she straddled me. This position would allow her to take as much of me as she was comfortable with, and I got to see every bit of pleasure written on her body and her face. Not to mention the way her tits bounced with every move.

With more restraint that I thought I had left, I raised my hips, and pulled her down, slowly, excruciatingly, and thrust into her. Her eyes drifted closed and she let her head fall back on her shoulders, her blonde hair drifting down her back, and she took my cock inch by inch.

"Mac, you feel so good. Give me more. I need all of you." Her eyelids fluttered, and she groaned as she sunk down onto me, taking me even deeper than before.

Our bodies fit together far too perfectly, and when she'd taken my entire shaft, her inner muscles squeezed and pulsated, sending jolts of intense pleasure through me. "All of me, for all of you."

I grabbed her hips, loving the feel of her plush, pillowy body in my hands, on my cock. Then I shifted my hips, letting her rise up, guided by my hands, then brought her back down, helping her fuck me.

And. Fuck. Me.

She licked her lips and whimpered as I bounced her on my cock faster and harder than before. "God, you're so deep. It feels so good. I need more. Don't stop."

"Don't worry, *Liebling*. I'm going to give you everything you need." My hips jerked, and I thrust into her. Her breasts and belly, hips and thighs, bounced and shook in such a gorgeous and sensual way that I wanted to touch and caress her everywhere, wanted my hands all over her at once.

She panted, and gasped for more breath, her nipples pearled into tight buds, and a flush crept up her chest and neck. Her body was clamoring to come, and she just needed a push to get over that edge into the bliss of orgasm, into oblivion.

She dropped her head down to look at me, and I reached up, gripping the back of her neck and pulled her down to me, never once letting up with the thrusts of my hips. She lost her rhythm entirely, and it was my turn to take control of her pleasure.

I slid my hands down her soft, sweet neck, wrapping my hands around, and finding those pulse points on either side of her throat. "That's right my naughty girl. I want you to come for me."

Her moans, turned into guttural groans, stuttering as I tightened my grip and pounded up into her. Her pussy clenched and released, then clamped down on me hard as she closed her eyes and exploded into her orgasm. I followed right behind, almost blacking out at the intensity of our matching climaxes.

Once we both came down out of that blissful high, she lay curled against my chest. I pulled her tighter against me and traced the ring on her finger. The diamond caught the city lights from our window, but it wasn't nearly as beautiful as Sara Jayne's smile.

"You really carried this around for weeks?" she asked, examining the vintage setting.

"I was waiting for the perfect moment." I pressed a kiss to her shoulder. "Though I didn't expect it to be a day where our goose gave game day predictions with The Boys for the Bowl, a viral scandal, and Tommy, of all people, saving the day."

"Sounds perfect to me." She turned in my arms, eyes sparkling. "But then again, I did get you to fake an engagement with me after knowing you for only like two days, so my judgment might be questionable."

"Best decision ever." I pulled her closer. "Both times."

The next morning, I needed about forty-two gallons of

coffee. I had a very busy night. But someone else beat me to the order at the hotel's little coffee shop.

"Two lattes, two rooibos beauty teas, one for me and one for the woman literally glowing with happiness, and —oh look," April grabbed the morning newspaper from the rack, and flipped right past the sports section and to the entertainment news. "The paper too, please. The Post already has your love story in print."

I stared down at the article with a snapshot of me and Sara Jayne being enveloped in a big hug from behind by MVP Tommy Frayzer. I'd have stood there all day if April hadn't nudged me to pick up our orders and guided me over to the booth at the hotel's coffee shop. Sara Jayne was there waiting with their baby girl in her arms, giving her a couple of bounces to keep her snoozing peacefully.

"Though I have to say." April glared at me and Sara Jayne as she distributed the beverages. "I'm a bit offended everyone's so shocked. It was obvious you two were madly in love from the moment I met you."

I nearly choked on my coffee. "Wait, what?"

"Oh, please." She waved her hand dismissively. "You two at Magda's party pretending to be engaged, then everyone thinks Sara Jayne's engaged to Tommy? I figured you were just trying to keep things private until you sorted out the whole house-sitting situation."

Sara Jayne stared at her. "You knew? This whole time?"

"Sweetheart, I've been married to football for fifteen years. I know when a player has fallen in true love when I see it." April's eyes sparkled. "Also, the way Mac looked at you... let's just say Tommy isn't the only one who needs acting lessons."

"Speaking of acting," Bridger said, joining us with Chris in tow, both clutching massive hot chocolates, "that was quite a performance at the press conference, Tommy."

Tommy grinned from his spot next to me. "What can I say? I'm a man of many talents."

"Like matchmaking?" April raised an eyebrow.

"And goose wrangling," Sara Jayne added. "Don't forget his true calling."

"About that..." Chris leaned forward eagerly. "We're having family game night next weekend. Dad says you should come because Sir Honksalot would have a lot of fun playing with all of us kids."

Bridger caught my eye with a knowing look. "Chris has been very insistent about expanding game night lately. Nothing to do with sweet little Trixie Moore moving in next door, I'm sure."

Chris turned as red as his hot chocolate cup. "Da-ad!"

"The plot thickens," Tommy stage-whispered. "Looks like I'm not the only matchmaker around."

"You guys have to come," Chris pressed on, desperately changing the subject. "Mac can tell me more about being an all-star quarterback for a division one level team, and Sara Jayne can help me with what to say to Trix... I mean, help us all with InstaSnap."

"Smooth," Bridger muttered into his coffee.

"We'd love to," I said, watching Sara Jayne try not to laugh at Chris's obvious crush. "Though Sir Honksalot's social media fee is getting pretty steep these days."

"I heard he's booked for a Valentine's day spread in that big home decor magazine," April said. "Something about trending holiday decorations?"

"Don't remind me." Sara Jayne showed them her phone, where #PorchGoose was still trending. "Apparently, we accidentally started a movement."

Tommy pulled up his own phone. "Ooh. I'm gonna need to order some V-day outfits for Honksy."

He tapped on his phone for a moment and then turned the screen toward me. "Wait. Have you seen the latest? People are recreating your love story. There's a couple who got engaged at a farm animal sanctuary where they've adopted a rescue goose."

"The internet is weird," Chris declared with all the wisdom of his thirteen years.

"But entertaining," Bridger added. "Christopher, I think Sir Honksalot is getting antsy. Go see if you can get him some snacks, will you?"

He waited until the teen trotted off and then looked over at the three of us with a slightly disapproving dad vibe. "Though the internet is not always, shall we say, factual. How much of Tommy's press conference story was actually true?"

"All of it," I said, squeezing Sara Jayne's hand. "Well, except the part about it being his master plan. He just got lucky that his chaos worked out."

"Excuse you," Tommy protested. "I am a strategic genius. Tell them, Sir Honks—" He stopped, looking around. "Where did Chris and our feathered friend get off to in the two whole seconds they were gone?"

Right on cue, a commotion erupted from the direction of the breakfast buffet. We turned to see Sir Honksalot waddling proudly back to our table, a stolen croissant in his beak and a trail of admirers with phones out behind him. Chris trailed behind with two more pastries in his hands.

"Some things never change," Sara Jayne laughed, then looked at me softly. "Thank goodness."

I kissed her, not caring who saw. We were done hiding anyway.

"Well," April said, "at least your wedding photos will be interesting."

They would be the best. Because they'd capture what would become my all-time favorite day ever. The day when Sara Jayne would become Sara Jayne Jerry. Forever my love, forever my life, forever my wife.

EPILOGUE: A VERY SERIOUS GOOSE

TEN YEARS LATER

Mac

The green room at the NFL draft buzzed with nervous energy, but Chris Kingman looked perfectly calm in his custom suit. Then again, being the son of legendary Coach Bridger Kingman probably helped prepare you for moments like this.

"Your tie's crooked," I said, more to have something to do with my hands than because it actually needed fixing.

Chris grinned, that same grin he had every time he won a game, or Footballopoly at Kingman family game. He knew he was hot shit, and so did every team in the league. I'd been on the phone with all the team owners from Detroit to Dallas and back again. They all wanted the hottest quarterback to win a college championship since... well since me. "You're looking as cocky as your Dad right now."

"It's not cocky if you know you're the best." Bridger

clapped a hand on my shoulder. "You've done enough deals for championship players to know that."

That I had.

We'd come full circle, somehow. From my own draft day dreams cut short by injury, to representing Tommy, to this moment—watching the kid who'd once begged me to tell him stories of my college football glory days about to get his own shot at the NFL.

"First pick's coming up," Chris said, checking his phone. "Tommy says the Mustangs' front office is suspiciously quiet."

"Tommy needs to stop trying to get insider information from the equipment manager," I laughed. Tommy would have the insider knowledge since he'd married that equipment manager. Only wedding I'd ever been to that was almost as great as mine. But honestly, any wedding party that included a goose, ranked right up there in my book.

The Mustangs had first pick, and Chris in Denver would be perfect. Too perfect, maybe. Because Lord knew Denver needed a comeback after the last couple of years of losing records. Manniway had won a couple of rings his first few years, but he needed to pass the torch now, and I couldn't think of anyone better to lead Denver into a new era of success than Christopher Bridger Kingman.

The NFL commissioner took the stage on the monitors. The room went quiet.

"With the first pick in the NFL draft," his voice boomed through the speakers, "the Denver Mustangs select... Christopher Kingman, Quarterback, Denver State University."

The room erupted. Chris hugged his father first, then me, then his father again. Cameras flashed. Someone handed him a Mustangs jersey with his name on it.

"Your mother," Bridger's voice was husky with emotion, "always said you'd play for Denver one day."

He slid the Mustang's hat onto Chris's head, but that didn't hide the glisten of tears in either of their eyes. "She knew, and she would have been so damn proud of you today."

Chris's smile turned gentle. "She always was."

"Ready?" I asked, as he prepared to walk out onto that stage.

He grinned again, pure joy and determination. "Born ready." He glanced at his phone. "Think we can get Sir Honksalot to do his touchdown dance at the press conference? For old time's sake?"

Some things, thankfully, never change.

Sara Jayne

"He's going to cry," Declan announced from his spot on the couch, phone already poised to capture his older brother's moment. "Chris always cries at big moments."

"Like you won't cry at your draft next year," Everett shot back, grabbing a handful of chips.

"I don't cry, I brood." Declan's attempt at a scowl was undermined by his obvious excitement. "It's my brand."

I settled deeper into my favorite armchair, taking in the controlled chaos of the Kingman living room. The twins, Flynn and Gryffen, were trying to teach Sir Honksalot a new touchdown dance, while Hayes and Isak argued about whether their brother would beat Johnston Manniway's stats in his first year on the team or not.

Jules perched on the arm of my chair, decked out in her Denver State jersey, fiercely debating with her Aunts May and June about their theory that Chris needed to start thinking about settling down.

"All I'm saying," May sighed, "is that now that he's going to be a big League star, Chris needs to find a nice girl to support him."

"Or maybe," Jules fired back, her young face so serious for a ten-year-old, "he needs to find someone whose dreams are just as big as his, and they can support each other."

"Ten going on thirty," June laughed.

May smiled too. "And just as hardheaded as her mother was."

Sir Honksalot chose that moment to waddle past with his latest prize—April's "In This House We Bleed Green" lucky pillow clutched triumphantly in his beak.

"How is he still stealing things at his age?" Isak wondered out loud.

"Don't be ageist, Isak." Jules chastised and then stuck her tongue out at him.

"Don't be a brat." Isak shot back.

Jules grinned and gave a little tip of her head, ready to deal her final blow. "I own that moniker proudly, thank you very much."

One would think they were bickering, but in the

Kingman family even teasing your siblings was a form of sport.

"It's simply dedication to his art," I replied, watching our mid-life goose arrange the pillow right in front of the TV and plop down on it, waiting for the results.

The commissioner took the stage on TV, and the room went almost silent. "That's mom's lucky pillow, so Chris has to go first now," Hayes whispered to me.

When the commissioner announced Chris's name and the Mustangs, the explosion of joy nearly knocked Sir Honksalot's carefully arranged pillow fort over.

"He's crying," Declan crowed, filming the TV. "Called it."

"Your brother just went first round to Denver," Aunt May wiped her own tears. "Of course he's crying. April would be so proud. Of all of you."

"Boys are allowed to show emotions." Jules said with absolute certainty, climbing into my lap. "And Mom's always proud of us. Even when the twins tried to teach Bear number two to play running back."

"That was one time," Flynn protested.

"This goose had more potential," Gryff added.

My phone buzzed with a text from Mac: *Coming home soon. Bringing the newest Mustang and his multi-million dollar deal. Sir Honksalot better dust off his old referee jersey.*

I smiled, remembering that first big bowl game so many years ago. Back then, I never could have imagined this life—being part of this beautiful, chaotic family, watching these kids grow up, building a life that was better than any fashion campaign.

Mac

The Kingman house erupted in cheers when Chris walked through the door. Sir Honksalot, not to be outdone, announced our arrival with his signature honk —still impressively loud, despite his age.

"There's my boy," His Aunt May pulled Chris into a hug while his Aunt June tried to fix his "TV hair."

"First-round draft pick and his hair's still a mess," June tsked.

"Some things never change," Bridger laughed, watching his oldest son get mobbed by his siblings.

"Uncle Tommy!" Jules squealed as Tommy and his husband Martine arrived with their twins, five-year-olds Jayne and Jerry, racing to join the chaos.

"Sorry we're late," Tommy grinned. "Someone had to make sure his tie was perfect for the photos."

"You're the one who spent twenty minutes fixing your hair," Martine countered, earning laughs from everyone who knew exactly how long Tommy took to get ready.

In the happy chaos of Tommy's kids teaching Sir Honksalot to dance to some new pop star who'd won a singing competition show they loved, while the Kingman boys argued over draft statistics, I found Sara Jayne watching it all with that soft and knowing smile I'd fallen in love with years ago.

"Pretty amazing family we ended up with," I murmured, wrapping my arms around her from behind.

She leaned back against me. "Better than anything we

could have planned." Her hand found mine. "Though I still can't believe Jerry asked Sir Honksalot to be his show-and-tell last week."

"That's our godson." I chuckled. "Following in his dad's footsteps with the goose-related chaos."

"Speaking of chaos," Sara Jayne nodded toward where Sir Honksalot was now waddling past with his newest prize—Chris's sock, somehow stolen despite his shoes being firmly tied.

"How does he do that?" Chris demanded. "I do not understand how people have birds as pets. They're nothing but trouble."

Tommy snorted. "That's what I said before Sir Honksalot changed my life." He scooped up little Jaynie who was trying to chase after the sock-stealing goose. "Though I have to admit, watching him teach my kids his tricks is a little concerning."

"He's just passing on his legacy," Martine said, catching Jerry before he could knock over Aunt May's carefully arranged celebration snacks.

I pulled Sara Jayne closer, thinking about legacies and family and how the best things in life rarely follow your carefully laid plans. We'd tried for years to have kids of our own, but somehow the universe had given us something different—and maybe even better. Seven honorary nephews who came to us for advice, one fierce little honorary niece who thought we hung the moon, two perfect godchildren, and a goose, while getting up there in fowl years, still thought sock theft was an Olympic sport.

"Wouldn't change a thing," Sara Jayne whispered, as if

reading my thoughts. "This is exactly the family we were meant to have."

Jules bounded over, Sir Honksalot trailing behind her with the sock still in his beak. "Uncle Mac, Aunt Sara Jayne, tell the story about the time Sir Honksalot made you fall in love."

"Oh no," Everett groaned. "Not the Oktoberfest story again. I'm telling you, chasing a goose or a girl is not the way to fall in love."

"Always the Oktoberfest story," Tommy grinned, settling on the couch with both twins. "It's a classic."

Later that night, after the celebration wound down, and we'd said our goodnights, I stood on the back porch of our Denver home watching Sir Honksalot arrange his stolen sock collection in the moonlight. Ten years, and he still treated every new acquisition like a precious treasure.

Mac's arms slipped around my waist. "Janynie wants to take him to kindergarten for Career Day."

"As what, exactly? A professional sock curator?"

"According to her very detailed plan, he's going to teach her class about 'being your authentic self, even if that self is a little chaotic.'" He chuckled against my hair. "Tommy swears Martine's the one who taught her that phrase."

"Smart kid." I leaned back against him. "Though I suppose Sir Honksalot did teach us all something about embracing our most authentic selves."

As if hearing his cue, our silly goose looked up from

his sock arrangement and let out a proud honk. The same honk that had started it all at Oktoberfest. The same honk that had approved our fake engagement and then our real one. The exact same honk that still announced every family gathering and holiday celebration.

Some people might think it's strange that a temperamental rescue goose with a sock-stealing habit changed our lives. That he led me to the love of my life, helped create a family bigger and more beautiful than we could have imagined, and somehow turned chaos into magic.

But then again, the best love stories usually are a little strange.

Just ask our silly goose.

Sir Honksalot

I conducted my nightly inspection of the neighborhood, waddling down the sidewalk, shaking my head, regally, of course, at the lack of proper porch decor. These homes were woefully under-goosed. Where was the elegant accessorizing? The artfully arranged chaos? The stolen sock displays?

Not that any decorative goose could match my natural gravitas. I had single-handedly or rather, single-wingedly, started the trend, after all. Though perhaps it was time for humans to branch out. Those roosters had potential— loud, opinionated, excellent at creating the kind of chaos that brought humans together.

Just look at what I'd accomplished with my humans.

Mac and Sara Jayne were clearly my finest work, though Tommy had been an excellent student in the art of controlled mayhem. And young Chris... well, I had plans for that boy. He just needed the right feathered companion to—

I stopped mid-waddle.

There, illuminated by moonlight in the Dawes's front yard, was the most beautiful goose I'd ever seen. Her feathers gleamed silver, her neck curved with impossible elegance, and she was rearranging the Dawes's garden gnomes with exquisite taste.

"You might try putting that one by the fountain," I honked before I could stop myself.

She turned, fixing me with eyes that sparkled with mischief. "I was thinking the same thing."

Her voice was like the soft splash of fountain water. "Why don't you come over and help me?"

I'd never waddled so fast in my life. "I'd be happy to, my lady...?"

"I'm Juliet. Juliet Montegoose."

My heart fluttered like a newborn gosling. Well, well. This was an unexpected turn of events. I'd spent a long time matchmaking for my silly humans.

Perhaps it was time for me to become a serious goose, and do a little matchmaking for myself. "It would be my pleasure. It's so very nice to meet you. I'm Sir Romeo Honksalot."

A NOTE FROM THE AUTHOR

Dear Reader,

pulls up comfy chair and pours us both a hot cocoa

Grab your cocoa (and maybe a croissant that hasn't been stolen by a certain feathered friend), because we're going to chat about how I felt compelled to pull a holiday novella out of my butt.

If you've read the other books in the Cocky Kingmans series, you might remember Mac, who is Chris's agent in *The C*ck Down the Block*, and his wife Sara Jayne, who has been a member of the Take Up Space Network from the beginning.

Sara Jayne is my plus-size queen who knows her worth and doesn't need anyone to validate her beauty. She's for every curvy girl who's been told to take up less space. Who's been passed over or pushed aside. She's my reminder that love stories are for everyone, no matter your size, shape, or what the scale says. And of course, that sometimes the best romance happens when you're completely, authentically yourself.

I thought it might be fun to see the origins of their story, which is why they became the perfect couple for this holiday novella. But... what kind of pet would they have? I'm serious when I tell you I'm running out of funny animal pet puns for titles!

And then I came across this wackadoodle thing called a porch goose! HAHAHAHAHAHA

If I had a porch, it would probably have at least three...or five...or a hundred goose statues dressed up in various costumes.

Everything about Sir Honksalot has cracked me up from the moment he hit the page. What's not to love about an opinionated waterfowl who thinks sock theft and matchmaking are Olympic sports. His character was inspired by the many rescue animals at my favorite sanctuary here in Colorado. Who despite difficult beginnings, have so much love to give. They just need someone to see past their rough edges—kind of like how Mac and Sara Jayne see past Tommy's "bad boy" reputation to the heart underneath.

Yes, yes I did suggest that Sir Honksalot started the whole porch goose trend. If you don't have one, why?

And then there's Tommy... When he first appeared on the page, I thought he was just that sort of douchpotatoey football bro. I just needed a lone problem client for Mac. I did not think he would become such an important part of Mac and Sara Jayne's story. But while writing this book, some important things changed in the world, that put the rights of LGBQT+IA people in serious jeopardy. If you're already a fan of mine, you know it's important to me to have not only body diversity in my stories, but all kinds of different people. Because that's the real, genuine world I live in, and I want that represented in the worlds I create in my mind.

Tommy's story is for everyone who's had to hide part of themselves to protect their dreams. But I also knew I had to give him a happy ever after too. So welcome to the found family of the Kingmans, Tommy.

A portion of the proceeds from this book will go to Lovin' Arms Animal sanctuary, because every Sir Honksalot deserves a chance at their own happily ever after. But another portion will go to the Trevor Project, because no one should have to be afraid to come out.

And finally, I want and need to tell you why this holiday novella exists at all. Look, friends, the world around us can be really dark sometimes. While we must continue to fight for our rights—for equality, for representation, for the simple dignity of being who we are—we also need moments of respite. We need self-care, solace, and safe spaces where we can escape and rejuvenate our souls.

That's why I decided to put out this holiday story set in the Kingmans world at the last minute. Because sometimes we all need a rescue goose who steals socks, a plus-size model who knows her worth, and a love story that reminds us joy exists even in chaos. I truly believe it's my vocation in this life to help bring joy into the world, one chaotic love story at a time.

Extra hugs from me to you,
—Amy

ACKNOWLEDGMENTS

I set everything else in my life aside to write this book. So I want to thank and acknowledge my friends and family for understanding when I can't come out and play. And for when they make me anyway.

I'm dedicating this book to my friend Sean who works so hard to help me be happy, healthy, and always believes in me. I want only happy ever afters for him forever. That and lots of cruises.

I so appreciate the author talks and days away from the computer at rando coffee shops around the Denver metro area with M. Guida, Holly Roberds, Parker Finch, and Nikki Hall. Y'all are my tribe.

Hugs to my 7-figure Diggers, Lucy Lennox, Hope Ford, and Kaci Rose. Thank you for being there for me (to compete with!)

Extra hugs to my curvy girl author friends, Kat Baxter, Stephanie Harrell, Molly O'Hare, Kelsie Stelting Hoss, Mary Warren, and Kayla Grosse. We're changing the world one fat-bottomed woman at a time, and I'm so grateful you're here fighting the good fight with me. I will ALWAYS continue to rec your books when anyone asks for romance with plus-size heroines, because I KNOW readers can trust their hearts with your positive fat rep!

I am ever grateful to my editor Chrisandra who

somehow still loves me and my stories, even though I will suck at commas and deadlines forever. Sorry. (But only a little bit.)

Thank you to Ellie at Love Notes PR for for quite literally helping me make my dreams come true. I can't wait to continue to SLAY with you for a long time to come.

Huge thanks to TheCaprica for drawing this amazing piece of art for the cover, and to Jacqueline Sweet for making it into the perfect cover.

So many hugs to my friends and PAs Kate Tilton, and Michelle Ziegler. My author life would be such a tangled mess with out you. I appreciate you more than you know.

And to my Patreon Book Dragons - you are the reason I write books. I hope I continue to entertain you and make you proud. Your continual support means so incredibly much to me. You make me smile and happy cry when I read your comments on the chapters.

For my Swoonies!

- Allie H.
- Amanda T.
- Allie H.
- Amanda T.
- Amber L.
- Angie M.
- Anna R.
- Anne-Marie P.
- Annmarie B.
- Billy O.
- Belinda M.

- Cathy G.
- Chanel S.
- Cheryl H.
- Crystal R.
- Dana G.
- Dawn J.
- Dominique R.
- Emily G.
- Essence C.
- Dominique R.
- Ilona T.
- Irehne A.
- Janna G.
- Jenna M.
- Jenny W.
- Jessica D.
- Johnna A.
- Judy R.
- Kasia R.
- Kat V.
- Kathryn B.
- Kathy B.
- Katrina D.
- Kayla M.
- Kaylee B.
- Kelley M.
- Kiarra C.
- Kyndal N.
- Laura B.
- Laura P.
- Lauren K.

- Leanna B.
- Macjenzie B.
- Maria B.
- McKaylee E.
- Monste R.
- Michelle A.
- Nicole C.
- Paige P.
- Pam G.
- Rebecca C.
- Rina H.
- Sami M.
- Sarah M.
- Shannon P.
- Sophie H.
- Stacey M.
- Stephanie J.
- Taisha F.
- Taylor M.
- Tiffany L.
- Treasure L.

For my VIP Fans!

- Amie N.
- Amy D.
- Angelique A.
- Angie K.
- Arabella L.
- Ashley B.
- Barb T.

- Brianna S.
- Cara-Lee D.
- Cate N.
- Christin C.
- Christy B.
- Diana B.
- Emily J.
- Kara C.
- Kerrie M.
- Kelli W.
- Kristin A.
- Lis T.
- Lisa W.
- Melissa E.
- Rachael C.
- Sara W.
- Shyann S.

For my Biggest Fans Ever, your support continually awes me. Thank you so much for believing in me.

- Alida H.
- Amy H.
- Ashley P.
- Bonnie M.
- Cherie S.
- Corinne A.
- Danielle T.
- Daphine G.
- Dawn B.
- Hana. K.

- Helena B.
- Kari S.
- Katherine M.
- Lisa W.
- Mari G.
- Megan F.
- Melissa L.
- Misty B.
- Orma M.
- RaeAnna F.
- Sandra A.
- Sandra B.
- Shannon B.
- Shardai B.
- Stephanie H.
- Stephanie F.
- Valeria L.

BEAR NAKED WITH THE BEARDED BALLER

INCLUDED IN THE CHASING HOLIDAY TAIL ANTHOLOGY

GET SNOWED-IN WITH LOVE

When plus-size model, April De la Reine, loses her agency and all her hopes for making a difference in the fashion world, she needs some peace and solitude to rethink her life. A cabin in the mountains of Colorado sounds like the perfect escape.

But her trip to the snowy wilderness of Bear Claw Valley gives her a dilapidated shack, a blizzard, a hilariously oversized dog as big as a bear, and the grumpy, bearded, and irresistibly infamous footballer, Bridger Kingman.

Stranded together in a snowed-in cabin, they soon discover that opposites do more than just attract and they find warmth in the best of places - each other's arms. 'Bear Naked with the Bearded Baller' is the steamy love-at-first-sight prequel to the Cocky Kingmans' series that will melt your heart, and your panties, no matter how cold the winter night.

CITIEST OF CITY SLICKERS

BRIDGER

*I*f I never signed another talent contract in my entire fucking life, it would be too damn soon. At this point, I didn't even want to see a football, much less hold one. I'd lived the sport for so long, loved it even, and all this media bullshit made me want to throw my TV and my *Sports Illustrated* subscription in the trash so I couldn't even watch a professional football game again, much less play in one.

Instead, I found myself driving through the winter wonderland of Bear Claw Valley, Colorado, the quaint small town where I grew up, wishing I could stay for longer than just the time off I had for our bye-week. I slammed the door of my faded red '67 Ford pickup truck, stomped up the sidewalk through the gravel and slush leftover from the last storm, and shoved my way into the Mayne hardware store. The familiar smell of pine and sawdust, layered with the sharp tang of winter, welcomed me home.

The bell above the door jingled in the way only a small

business in a quaint country town could. A poster for my local Cause for Paws charity event that was happening next weekend hung by the entrance. I'd take the sound of that bell over the ringing of my phone any day, all day, twice on Sundays. I made my way through the familiar aisles, not needing a damn thing except the peace and quiet.

I nodded to Tex behind the counter, who was busy flipping through the pages of a catalogue. He gave a chin jerk response. "Kingman."

That's what I liked about him. He didn't blather on and on and on and on like some people I knew. Like my fucking agent.

I glanced at the new display from Husqvarna, because I needed a new chainsaw as much as a hole in my ass, then headed over to the lumber section. The scent of sawdust and fresh cut pine seeped in, better than any icy-hot muscle rub down from a trainer. I took my first full, deep breath in an hour. My work boots scuffed against the linoleum floor, and I shoved my hands in my pockets, scowling at the options in front of me.

Both the wood and my career.

I was about to grab a few castoffs I could carve up when I caught sight of something hot pink and furry, out of the corner of my eye. The scent of orange, vanilla, and sweet cinnamon wafted over and went straight to my cock.

My days of adrenaline fucking were over. But man, a good railing, up against a wall, making a woman scream my name as I pounded into her... I told my libido to cool it. I was not good company right now. Even the media knew that. Since I'd just been named the league's meanest player.

I stared through the shelves anyway and found my feet shifting toward the tempting sex-on-a-stick. She was an aisle over, her basket filled with an odd collection of items — paint brushes, a bag of nails, a roll of duct tape, and a trowel. I couldn't begin to imagine what she was planning to do with all those items.

I stepped into the aisle full of small tools she was perusing and fu-uck. She was no stick. Sexy cinnamon roll more like it. Tits I could get lost in, an ass that didn't quit, hips I wouldn't break if I grabbed on tight while fucking her, and thick thighs I wanted to use as earmuffs.

She wasn't a Colorado mountain girl, that much was clear from her outfit. Maybe she'd fit in with the kind of people who lived in Aspen. Nobody in Bear Claw Valley would be caught dead in fake leopard fur trim on a coat that didn't look like it would hold up to forty-degree weather, much less forty below. And those boots. While I'd like to see her in nothing but those black shiny knee-highs, heels weren't exactly good for the snow.

She moved from section to section, her gaze flitting over the items, grabbing all kinds of random shit. And I turned into a god-forsaken stalker, watching her, lusting after her.

Just say something to her, creeper.

It wasn't like I didn't know how to talk to women. I'd charmed my fair share of ball bunnies. But I didn't have a clue what to say to Cinnamon Roll.

Can I taste your ooey gooey sweet center was not a good pick-up line.

She paused and turned toward me, so I reached for a roll of wallpaper. Pale pink with little unicorns on it, as it happened. I examined those unicorns like they were the San Francisco offensive line. I kept my eyes glued to the paper so hard, I didn't even move until something jolted against my foot. I glanced down to see the woman's overflowing basket tipping over, dumping half the contents onto my feet as she squatted and reached for something on the very back of the bottom shelf.

Her jacket rose up her back, and the waistband of her ridiculous black suede pants gaped so that I got a clear view of the intricate tattoo scrawled across her lower back. A unicorn. A god-damned fucking unicorn prancing in some kind of magical sunlight.

Holy hell. There was no talking my cock down this time. The second she looked up, she was going to get a load of the pop-up tent in my jeans.

"Watch where you're going," I ground out and tried to step around, over, away from her, practically falling all over myself.

The deepest sky blue eyes, framed with long, dark lashes, stared up at me. She didn't seem fazed by my attitude or my hard-on that was practically in her face. Instead she smiled sweetly. "Oh, so sorry. I thought you might need this gold trim paint to go with your pink unicorn wallpaper. Excellent choice, by the way. Is it for you? Or maybe your girlfriend, wife, daughter? Please tell me it's for dear old Granny's kitchen remodel."

Her eyes sparkled up at me. They fucking sparkled.

I was a dead man.

She was fishing to see if I was single, and I had absolutely no response. Even my own name escaped me at the moment. Sweet baby Jesus, what was my name?

Cinnamon Roll stood, straightened her jacket, and held out her hand. "I'm new in town, and I'm trying to fix up my cabin up in the mountains, but I don't know what I'm doing. You don't happen to be a contractor who could help or know of one I could hire?"

My brain turned back on and piqued at the mention of the cabin. "What cabin?"

"Up on Bear Claw Mountain."

That's where I lived. Who in the hell sold a chunk of the Bear Claw to a city slicker? She had the tiniest hint of a Texas twang, and I had an idea who'd given her that land. "Up at the top?"

She smiled like I'd just guessed her favorite flavor of ice cream. "The very tippy top."

That was no place for a city girl like her. How would she even get herself up there? She looked like she drove a Mercedes, not a four-wheeler. I knew that cabin, or rather that dilapidated pile of wood. It was just above my plot and accessible by four-wheel drive only. Windy as hell, and had the absolute best view of the valley.

I looked her up and down, studying her, trying to decide whether she was a liability or not. Attractive, I'd give her that, but she was an outsider. Playing at living a simple life. In reality, she probably loved the tabloids and some ripe gossip. Someone for me to stay far away from.

Walk away, dumbass. I leaned in. "That cabin isn't far from me. What are your plans for it?"

"I want to fix it up and make it a sustainable, beautiful space to get away from it all." She sighed and I could practically see her mountain cabin fantasy floating around her head. "I'm hoping to use local and reclaimed wood as much as possible and make it energy efficient. Maybe get some solar panels in and—"

Had she even seen the place? And why wasn't I walking fast and far from this whole conversation? My head yelled run, but everything else below the neck, and especially below the waist, said stay awhile. See where this goes. "What kind of features you planning?"

"Well, I want to have a big fireplace, for the cold nights." She got this adorable, dreamy look on her face that had me imagining things too. Although, my fantasies were more about what I could do with her in front of that fireplace on a chilly night.

"I also want to have a big kitchen, for entertaining, and a big porch to enjoy the views and the fresh air. Ooh, and also a green roof, a place where I can grow plants and maybe attract some animal friends."

I'd be her animal friend.

Gah. No. I wouldn't. Getting involved with a woman like this was the absolute last thing I needed. She was high maintenance and I barely maintained myself these days. Being with her would draw a lot of attention. I just wanted the world to leave me the fuck alone.

The cabin she'd bought was no bigger than a hundred, maybe a hundred and fifty square feet. It was one room with a loft. She wasn't getting her big kitchen or entertaining space. So, not sure why I didn't bring that up. "That sounds like a big project, have you thought about the insulation, or the roofing?"

Shut up, Kingman. Shut the fuck up and walk away.

Tex poked his head into the aisle where we were standing, and I was absolutely using him to escape. "Hey, April. Lumber's ready. Come on up to check out. Kingman, you leave my customers alone, you grump."

Hmm. Yeah. The way Tex was all casual with her, he knew her. I gave him the bird.

"Thanks, Tanner. Yay." She gave him a sparkling smile and I glared at him.

April. That suited her. She was like springtime come to life. All sunshiny and gonna make a big muddy mess of my life. I'd be smart to freeze her out right now.

Instead, I was fucking thawing from the stone cold winter of the soul I'd sunk into. Hell.

She picked up her basket and I bent and grabbed the duct tape that was trying to roll away. "I think you're gonna need more than duct tape to fix up that old cabin."

April took the tape from me and lingered a long time with her fingers on mine. "If you can't fix it with duct tape, it can't be fixed."

Now if that wasn't the hottest thing I'd ever fucking heard, I don't know what was. I watched her walk away, partly to see that ass sway and mostly because I needed a minute to talk my hard-on down so I didn't embarrass myself in front of the entire town.

That was press I didn't need.

I waited until I heard the jingle of the door, all the while thinking of baseball, the Queen of England, and how Henry David Thoreau had made *Walden* so dang boring when it could have been great. All of that cooled my raging lust for a woman I'd barely talked to enough that I could go grill Tex about her.

He was already back to flipping through his dog-eared power tool catalog.

"You sold April the top of the Bear Claw, didn't you?" They were probably from the same small hometown back in Texas or something. How else would a Texan like her find out about a piece of property that wasn't for sale unless you knew who to talk to, sixteen hundred miles away.

Colorado was going to be a culture shock.

"Yep." He flipped another page and wasn't going to say another damn word. I could wait him out.

I stood there for a good three minutes while he flipped the pages. Dammit. His silence broke me like a rookie looking for praise from his coach. Tex didn't even look up.

"She can't fix that place up herself. You saw her shoes." She'd break her ankle the minute she walked out the front door. Probably while walking to the door. Then I'd have to go on up there and...

Page flip. "You gonna help her?"

Me? No. What? No. "Not a fucking chance. She'll sell it and never come back soon enough when she realizes she doesn't know what she's doing."

"Maybe." Tex shut the catalogue and looked right at me. "Or maybe she's tougher than she seems."

I'd believe that when I saw it. I'd better hike on up to her place and make sure she wasn't about to freeze to death stuck in a snowbank or something. I'd pull her plump ass out of the snow, then I'd take her back to my place and warm her right up.

Dammit. No. I needed to pretend I'd never even met

her. I had plenty of other things to worry about, like my own fucked up career, and the Cause for Paws event this weekend. I had one fucking weekend off before we played our last game, and I wasn't wasting my bye-week on some fling. Unless April was some kind of PR-nightmare-fix-it girl, I didn't need her complicating my life.

Complicating my bed, maybe.

Hell, that was tempting.

BEARS DON'T TALK

APRIL

"You have no new messages." Sigh. Of course I haven't missed any calls, because not one magazine, website, or even catalogue was booking plus-size models. Every brand was into heroin chic, and I hated that with all my heart.

Not that I had any models left to book. All my girls had given up.

I should have been a sports agent like my daddy. The money to be made there didn't care what your body looked like, just if you could play. In fact, the football teams slathered like drooling St. Bernards over big, thick linebackers. Like Bridger Kingman.

I'd admit to a little of my own drooling. He was one hell of a big boy, and I hadn't missed the big boy tenting the front of his pants either. You'd have to be on the fricking moon not to see that, and I had been eye to umm, eye with his... oh geez, I needed to quit thinking about him in that way. Totally inappropriate.

Yeah, I'd known who he was the moment I saw him

pick up that unicorn wallpaper. You'd have to be living under a rock, in a cave, with no cell phone reception to miss professional football's meanest defensive linebacker.

Word on the street was that he was about to fire his agent and was a giant pain in the ass to work with. Regardless, everyone in the biz would be climbing over each other to get him signed. Who wouldn't with a multimillion-dollar contract on the line? Good luck to them.

He didn't seem that mean to me. Maybe a bit distracted and grumpy, but his eyes had sparkled when he'd asked me about my cabin.

My. Cabin.

All I'd wanted was someplace to get away from the hustle and bustle of New York, but someplace far, far away from Texas and the disappointment I knew was waiting from my parents. I needed some peace and quiet to regroup and figure out what in the world I was going to do next.

When I emailed Tanner, my sister May's brother-in-law, asking if he had a lead on someplace in the mountains where he lived that I could escape to, he'd somehow talked me into buying this cabin.

As my rented SUV slipped and skidded through the snow on the one-lane barely-a-road for the eleventy-hundredth time, I was beginning to understand why I'd gotten such a great deal. I should be able to see the place by now, but all I saw were more trees and over there, some more trees, and up there, even more trees. Oh, and then there were the rocks.

My tires spun and I moved a half an inch or so forward. I really should pay more attention to where I was driving and quit daydreaming about how I'd like to see the monster in Bridger Kingman's pants for myself.

"Come on, four-wheel-drive, you can do it. I promise a nice long rest for you if you just get me to the cabin, okay?" I didn't dare go any faster than I already was, but at this rate, I'd be lucky to get to the top of the mountain by sunset.

What if there were wild animals in the dark waiting to eat me? Tanner had said there were bears in this area. I gave the SUV a bit more gas and prayed I didn't end up a story in the newspaper. "Failed plus-size model turned talent agent dies in mysterious car accident. Did she see that tree coming? More news at eleven."

I skidded around in the snow some more and happily avoided plowing into any trees. But then the road just ended, and there, within the dusky rays of sun shining down through the clouds, was my cabin.

Or, err, my wooden shed? Damn. This place had sure looked bigger in the pictures. The pile of wood Tanner had promised would be stacked next to it was as tall as, and almost as wide as, the whole building itself. That's what I got for buying it sight unseen.

Two minutes after I opened the door, I knew I was screwed. It was colder inside than out, and I had no idea where to even start. The right answer was probably to go home. To Texas.

A fire. I'd start with a fire. There was enough junk and leaves and stuff tossed around in here to burn down the forest. I should burn the whole cabin down and start from scratch. What a pile of poop Tanner had sold me. He was getting an earful from me tomorrow, and then I was tattling on him to my sister.

I blew out a long breath and rubbed my hands together. I was not a quitter. I could still do this if it meant the peace and quiet I needed to rethink my life. Step one, start a fire to warm the place up, step two was going to be cleaning up and a bit of inventory to see if I even had a place to sleep tonight. Besides my car. Did Bear Claw Valley even have a hotel? I'd even take a motel at this point.

Nope. No. That was prissy quitter thinking, and I was not giving up.

I grabbed some logs from the pile of wood outside, some newspapers from the stack next to the little wood-burning stove, and the long matches out of the bag of stuff I'd bought at the hardware store. I'd gotten them hoping to light some scented candles, not even thinking I'd need them to survive the night.

I could always drive back down the mountain, but I could not take another defeat just yet. First, I was calling on my finely honed Girl Scout skills and doing the best with what I had in front of me. Twelve matches and two slightly singed fingers later, and I had a fire going. And only half the cabin had filled with smoke before I figured out how to open the damper to the flue.

Step one down, a million more to go if I was going to make this into my ideal retreat. I hadn't bought a broom, but I did get a little dustpan and brush. Good thing there was only about a hundred square feet of floor.

I started piling up the junk near the door, found a half-full bottle of whiskey for my trouble, and discovered the chain that was supposed to be attached to the pull-down ladder to the little sleeping loft. I was looking around for something I could stand on to reattach it when I heard the scratching and growling at the door.

Crap. I knew I was going to get eaten by a wild animal.

No, no. Calm down. Maybe it's just a squirrel, or a raccoon. I wanted to make animal friends. I'd just go peek out the window and see what had come to visit. Granted, I could barely see out of the dirt crusting the panes, but that meant whatever was out there wouldn't be able to see me either.

Still, I bent over and sneaky-style creeped to the window and peeked over the ledge.

Oh my gawd. There was something big and brown and furry sniffing around the door.

A bear. There was a freaking bear trying to get into my cabin. A freaking bear.

I dropped down to my knees so it couldn't see me. Maybe if I stayed very quiet, it would go away. But wait, didn't bears have an excellent sense of smell? Oh no. What if I smelled delicious?

Very carefully, I crawled across the floor to the opposite wall. Geez, the floor was absolutely freezing. Frigid air poured up through the boards. If the air could get in, it meant it could get out, and that meant the bear would smell me anywhere.

Think, April. Think of a solution.

If it can't be fixed with duct tape, it can't be fixed.

I crawled over near the stove and pulled the big, silvery roll of tape out, snapped the plastic wrapping open with my teeth and very, very gently pulled an arm's length off the roll. Any faster, and I risked the bear hearing a sound that could very well be interpreted as a growl, or the cry of an injured... umm, bunny?

The bear scratched at the door again, and I swear I heard snuffling sounds. It took everything I had to hold in my squeaks of fear.

What if I duct taped the door shut? Surely a mass of sticky tape would flummox a wild animal. I put the piece of tape with my teeth and crawled back toward the door. If I paid attention to the cardio workout level of my heartbeat or the tangy taste of fear in the back of my throat, I wouldn't get this done.

Carefully I laid the tape across the bottom of the door —where I could literally see his feet moving around in the gap—and pressed the edges to get it to stick. This piece was only long enough to go halfway.

Before I got another piece started, the bear jumped up on the door and the whole cabin rattled, the door quaking on its hinges. I couldn't help it this time, the scream just popped out of me. In response I heard a horrible woofing sound. I didn't know bears sounded like dogs.

"Go away. I'm sure I'm not delicious to eat." Which was a lie. I had plenty of fat stores that I'm sure a bear would relish. Wasn't he supposed to be hibernating?

"Bear, you get back down here, you naughty thing. Just because you're cute, doesn't mean you can—" A grouchy, deep, manly voice yelled at the animal from somewhere near the cabin. I was saved.

Wait a minute. Bears don't talk. And who talks to bears? Especially like that? I knew just the grumpity grump who had the balls to yell at a bear.

"Help. I'm being attacked by a wild animal!" Oh geez, I hoped that didn't anger the beast and have it knocking down my door to eat my face.

"Down, Bear. Sit."

I listened close to try and see what in the world would happen next. Surely a bear doesn't follow commands. Then I heard the slurping and chomping sounds. Crunch, cronch, crack.

Oh no. Oh, no no no no no. The bear was eating Bridger and it was all my fault.

"Good boy. That's a good boy, you're the best boy, aren't you, Bear? Yes, you are." The sweetest ooey gooey voice praised the bear.

Like... what?

First of all, Bridger Kingman didn't know how to be sweet, and second, did he have a trained bear? This wasn't the eighteenth-century Russian court for goodness' sake, it was a small mountain town in Colorado.

Someone, or something, knocked on the door, practically rattling it right off the hinges. "April? It's Bridger Kingman. We met at the hardware store. You're okay now. Come on out. No one's going to eat you."

Swear to God, I heard him mumble something more that sounded like, "Unless you ask me too."

I crawled back across the floor and peeked over the windowsill. Yep. That was Bridger Kingman, petting the fluffy, brown, furry head of his... dog.

His. Big ass, brown, fluffy, furry dog.

I slipped down the wall and hung my head for a full three breaths while I made faces at myself. It took me a couple more to tell my heart to stop freaking out. No bears were going to eat me. But maybe a hot defensive linebacker was?

It's not like every woman I knew didn't have a crush on him. Well, no. That wasn't entirely true. New York's elite chic, who were literally scared of large bodies, didn't go gah-gah for him. Bridger was a big boy. Had to be for his job.

And that turned me the hell on. What I wouldn't do to be wrapped up and kept safe and warm by someone who wasn't going to break when I sat on their face.

Did it just get hot in here? I fanned my face and then remembered Bridger was literally standing at my door asking for me. Right. I was hot from embarrassment, not because I was fantasizing about what that beard could to do my girly parts.

Get your poop in a group, April. The man is standing at your door. Open it.

I pulled myself off the floor and gave the handle a tug. It moved but was stuck. Oh, right. I taped it shut. A good yank, and the door opened. The duct tape went flying and stuck to my leg, all twisted up. "Sup?"

Sup? Really? That's what I decided to say? Okay then, let's go with white girl gangsta style. "Yo."

Bridger looked down at his dog who made that cute head twist dogs make when they don't know what's happening either. I couldn't blame him. I didn't know what I was going on right now.

"Uh, yo... uh, you doing okay up here?"

"Yep, fine. Super, great. Can't you tell?" I waved my hand around the wreck of a cabin.

"I can. Bear decided he wanted to check out the new

neighbor, and I figured we'd better make sure this old cabin wasn't falling down around you."

The steps to the little loft came crashing down just as he said that. I cringed and sank down into myself and squeaked, "Everything's fine."

"Right. Well, there's a storm coming, and—"

Just as he said that, not one, not two, not three, but three billion snowflakes crashed down from the sky. I thought snow was supposed to come down all floaty and pretty. This was not pretty. It was snowpocalypse.

I grabbed Bridger by the front of his shirt and yanked him into the cabin. He tripped over the other twisted piece of duct tape and grabbed onto me to stay upright.

Which meant I ended up curled into his great big bear-hug arms. What was that he said about eating me if I asked?

FALLING IN A SNOWSTORM

BRIDGER

*S*hould I tell her now that she had duct tape covered in bits of leaves stuck in her hair? Or that she had a smear of dust across the bridge of her nose like the cutest smattering of fake freckles? Probably not.

"You've, uh, got something right here." I reached out and rubbed my thumb across her cheek, and then found myself cupping her chin and tilting her face up so I could stare into those sparkling eyes.

Her lips parted just the tiniest bit, and her tongue peeked out, wetting her lips. "Oh, do I? I'm sure I'm a mess."

The hottest fucking mess I'd ever met.

I was not a mess kind of guy. Until my agent flipped my whole damn career upside down by committing me to four more years with the worst team in the league, my life was ordered and predictable. Work hard, play hard, rest hard. Make a plan and stick to it to get what you want.

My gaze flicked down to her lips and back up. "Yeah, you are. Do you want me to help you?"

What the fuck was I saying? I just came up here chasing after Bear. Figured I should check on the city slicker to make sure she wasn't being stupid.

There was a storm coming, and since I knew good and well this cabin wasn't severe weather ready, it wasn't like I was going to let her ride out the night with the wind blowing through this place and freezing her to death.

"I think mother nature is going to insist." April glanced outside and I turned my head to see what she was seeing.

Holy shit. That storm rolled in quick. I'd thought I tell her to head into town and get a room at our little B&B. But it was looking like Bear and I were going to be stuck up here in this disaster. We were going to die if I didn't do something right quick to make sure we didn't.

So I did the best thing I knew to warm up. I kissed April.

The moment my lips touched hers, there were no chills to be found. I licked along the seam of her lips and the snowy mountains turned into volcanoes. Our tongues slid against each other, and the polar fucking ice caps melted. She moaned into my mouth and the Earth turned into the surface of the sun.

But it was her soft whimper as I deepened the kiss further, exploring every part of her mouth with my own, that melted my god damned socks off.

April gripped my shirt and slipped her hands into my hair. She was no shy, wilting flower waiting for my mouth and tongue to take hers. She gave as good as she was getting.

By the time we broke apart, both gasping for air, I

think she'd counted every one of my teeth and my tonsils with her tongue as her guide.

She blinked slowly as if waking from a long, languid nap, and damn if I didn't want to see what she actually looked like waking up in my arms. "If your plan was to distract me from the fact that your dog is actually a bear and we're about to be stuck in a snowstorm with only a chocolate candy bar, a half bottle of whiskey I found, and that tiny stove for heat, umm, it worked."

"That was exactly my plan. How did you guess?" I hadn't come up here with the intention to do anything but check that she was safe and prepared for the storm. "But also, we should probably at least shut the door so we don't actually freeze to death."

Neither of us moved. I didn't want to let her go. It was like she had a spell on me, and I didn't mind one bit.

Wait, what had she said about not having supplies? Damn. I knew she wasn't prepared. I was going to murder Tex later for selling her this place and not making sure she didn't die up here on the mountain. "No food or water?"

She smiled lazily, not concerned even a little bit. "Can one survive on kisses alone?"

Yes.

Dammit. No. But I was going to die trying.

No, no I wasn't. We could kiss and hopefully do lots more from the warmth and safety of my cabin. "Get your coat on. We'll hike back down to my place."

She glanced out the door, then back at me, and out the door again. "Umm. I am wearing my coat."

Shit. I glanced around the room to see if there was an

old blanket lying around or something we could wrap her in. The wind chill was going to be brutal. No way I was letting her get frostbite. "I suppose those are the best shoes you have?"

"I guess I'm not very well prepared. I've never spent a lot of time anyplace that it snows. I didn't know it would be quite so cold or happen so fast." She gave me a chagrined smirk. "Well, there are some fuzzy slippers in my suitcase."

This was about to be a fucking survival situation so I absolutely should not be imagining her in nothing but those slippers. Get your head in the game, Kingman. "If you've got flannel pjs in there too, we'll take it. But we've got to move before the snow starts drifting. It's not that far. Come on."

"No chance we can drive? My rental has seat heaters, which are heaven on a tight back."

"Can't get there from here. No road between my place and yours. Just a trail. The visibility is going down quick, and we'd have to drive all the way down the mountain to get you anywhere else safe. I think a quick hike is our best bet."

The kind of hike that would get icy and slippery and someone wearing heels could break an ankle. We'd just have to hold hands the whole way so I could make sure she stayed upright.

April made a face like what we were about to do was the worst idea ever, and she wasn't entirely wrong. I zipped up her coat and expertly wrapped my scarf around her neck, ensuring every bit of exposed skin was covered.

I wanted to be able to savor that skin later, and I

couldn't do that if she got frostbite. It would be a damn shame if that soft spot in the small of her throat turned blue.

I slipped my own gloves onto her little hands, and had to keep myself from growling, irritated that she wasn't already wrapped up in blankets, in front of the rolling fireplace, wearing nothing but a smile.

"Mrph mrr mss." Her words were muffled through the scarf.

I pulled one inch of it down. "What?"

"Let's do this."

I gave her a quick nod and took her hand in mine, leading her and Bear out into the fucking blizzard.

The sharp gusts of snow stung our faces, swirling around us. April's boots no sooner left the interior of her cabin than she was sinking into the soft folds of powder. A few steps past her car, and I couldn't see her feet. It was a good fucking thing I'd walked this trail a billion times over the years.

Each and every step we took, she nearly toppled over. But she gripped my hand tight, and there was no way I was letting her veer off the path.

But then the wind picked up and every flake of snow that had accumulated on the mountain for the last ten years swirled around us. I could barely see two feet in front of my face. But I could see Bear's big old wagging tail. He loved a good snowstorm, this was like his playground.

I squeezed April's hand. It was hard to talk in this wind and she hadn't said a word since we started walking. "We're almost there. Just a few more minutes."

She nodded, but her eyes were about as big around as my biceps. I hated that she was scared. I didn't even know this woman, so I shouldn't have a pounding behind my heart wanting to make everything right with the world for her.

Another hundred yards, and my cabin was finally in sight, its inviting light glowing through the snowflakes. I pointed and her tight shoulders went from up around her ears back to normal as she let some of her worry go. She pulled down the scarf and blew out a long steamy breath. "It's so cute. Not what I'd expect for a big growly dude like you."

She shook her head back and forth, let go of my hand and pressed a glove to her face, her eyes doing a dance of confusion. "My nose hairs are frozen. Is that even a thing? How—"

She was the one that was cute. My cabin was average. Before I could even tell her so, April slipped, her body vanishing beneath a thick white blanket of fluffy wet and cold snowflakes. My whole body went heavy and still like rocks as I watched April slip beneath the snow. Bear dove in, snuffling all around, clearing the area all surrounding her. He barked at me like he was saying, "hurry up and save her, dummy."

I stumbled towards her, my hands trembling as I scooped through the snow. She reached up for me, and I pulled her up and straight into my arms, picking her up like a rescued princess. The fear intertwined with a strange sense of familiarity as I held her against my chest, as if I had done it a thousand times before.

She squealed and wrapped her arms around my neck. As if I'd ever drop her.

I took long strides, carrying her like some kind of Victorian romance heroine who needed rescuing. I was no Mr. Willoughby, but I was a linebacker and I rushed up the stairs and through the door of the cabin like I was scoring a touchdown.

Bear followed us in, and I kicked the door shut, taking a deep breath and soaking up the heat. He went straight into the kitchen and curled up in his plush bed next to the water heater. He'd never be the curl up in front of the fireplace dog. Not since the forest fire he'd been rescued from as a pup.

April's teeth clattered and I set her back on her feet in front of the fire, but still holding her in my arms, not wanting to let go just yet. Some stray strands of hair begged my fingers to brush them away from her forehead, and I couldn't resist one more soft touch before I set to getting her warm. The protective instincts I didn't even realize I had for her had not just kicked in, they were kicking my ass.

April was mine. She belonged with me, and I wanted nothing more than to be hers.

But this was too fast. No one fell in love after one meeting and a hike down a mountain in a snowstorm. Not in real life anyway.

She looked up at me like I was her hero. I wanted to be.

"Good thing you're the biggest man I've ever met in my life." Her voice came out soft and breathy. "I'm not sure I'd trust anyone else to pick me up and carry me like that."

Her arms were still wrapped around my shoulders, and I wasn't moving an inch. "You should be carried everywhere."

That sounded like I was chastising her, and I cursed my tongue for being such a grump. I'd been cranky with everyone around me for so long, I wasn't sure I knew how to talk any other way.

I'd do it again right now and carry her to my bed if she'd let me. I swallowed hard and cleared my throat. "We should get you warmed up."

"Yes, we should." She pulled off the gloves I'd put on her and reached for the zipper of my jacket. "With body heat. Lots and lots of shared body heat."

April's naughty little grin melted my icy fucking heart in more ways than one. For the first time in what felt like a thousand years, the corners of my mouth turned up in a genuine smile. Not because I was about to get laid—not that I was sad about that. But because I'd found someone who made me want to be happy.

That smile on my face grew as I reached for her jacket too. "Yep. Everyone knows that's the best way to get warm. I'm practically hot already."

April giggled, and it went first to my soul, and then straight to my cock. "Ooh, I wanna be hot."

"You are so fucking hot." That just slipped out and I wasn't sorry.

April blushed and I couldn't wait to do that to every inch of her skin from head to toe and everywhere in between.

THE HOTTEST SNOWPOCALYPSE

APRIL

I gazed up into Bridger's eyes, and anticipation bubbled up inside me. Our bodies were so close that his hot breath washed over my skin. That smile of his did something fun and naughty to my lower belly. And so did his dark eyes, glimmering with desire, hidden cleverly beneath thick lashes. Delicious.

I didn't always trust men with my body. Especially in New York and L.A. where it felt like the only way to exist was heroin chic. I wanted to prove that curves and thick thighs and soft bodies were beautiful and worthy of being worshipped too.

My failed talent agency had made me doubt that.

Bridger's absolute lust for me both in this moment and when we'd kissed up at my cabin, helped me remember. I could read the truth in him. He wasn't faking any bit of this heat radiating between us just to get his dick wet. He was hot for me, and that right there made me trust him so much more than I had anyone else in my love life.

Jumping into bed with someone I'd met just a few

hours ago wasn't something I'd ever done before, and I likely wouldn't ever do again.

Aside from the whole *we didn't die in a snowpocalypse so let's prove to the universe just how alive we are* thing, there was something about him that was just... right. Right for me. I felt that at a gut level, and I couldn't wait to get to know him better to see what truth there was to that instinct. After we fucked each other's brains out.

This was going to be lots of fun. I grabbed hold of his shirt and tugged it open so the buttons went flying. With a quick yank of his collar, I pulled him tight against me, our lips mere centimeters apart.

A claim I'd longed to say to the right man, came easily with Bridger. I mouthed the words against his lips. "You belong to me, big boy."

He chuckled, his amber eyes twinkling in the firelight. I ran my hands along the hard planes of his chest and felt his muscles ripple beneath my touch.

"Say it again," he commanded. His voice was low and seductive, like dark honey drizzling over me.

"You. Belong. To me," I breathed against his mouth, feeling out of control in all the best kinds of ways.

His lips brushed against mine and he growled out his reply, "And you're mine now too."

He yanked my coat off my arms and tossed it aside, then slipped his hands under the hem of my sweater to pull it over my head. I expected his fingers to be cold, but his touch seared me as he slid the material up and over my head. When my head popped out, he waggled his eyebrows at me and trapped my arms in the sweater, holding them over my head, forcing me to arch my back.

With an entirely too-delicious sparkle in his eye, he backed me up against the wall next to the fireplace and trapped me there with his big, strong body.

"I've been dying to taste this particular spot of skin since the moment I saw you." His hand roamed across my waist, then up and up, learning every single nook and cranny of my curves. Shivers went down to my toes, and I leaned into his touch.

"That's not one spot." The words came out in a gasp as he skimmed his knuckles over my bra and across the tops of my breasts, not giving me half of what I wanted. Tease.

"I want to taste all of you."

Bridger bent his head and pressed his lips to the spot his fingers had just been. Instead of a soft kiss, he scraped his teeth across my skin, nipped at me, and then kissed away the sting.

My breath hitched, and I groaned out at every new sensation that crashed through me. "Then taste me. All of me."

"You are so damn beautiful. Every inch of you." He whispered these sweet nothings, punctuated with soft kisses and little nips all up and down my throat.

I was a model. I knew I was beautiful, even when what felt like the rest of the world didn't. But when he said it, his words empowered me in a way that had me feeling so alive in this moment. With him, and only him, the binds of any inhibitions or doubts that were holding me back broke, and I was free.

He finally yanked the sweater from my hands and tossed it aside. His fingers went to the back of my neck, and he threaded them through my hair. We stared into each other's eyes so long, I was sure I'd fallen into a sexy dream.

His eyes flicked from mine down to my lips and stayed there. I didn't want to break this spell, but I also couldn't wait for him to kiss me again. I parted my lips on my next breath and tilted my chin up, leaning into him, needing him to meet me the other fifty percent of the way.

Just before he leaned in, he looked so deeply into my eyes as if he wanted to dive into the depths of who I was, and at that moment, all I could think about was how perfect it felt when we were together like this.

We were two souls meeting for the first time, discovering something more powerful than either one of us had ever imagined possible. The look on his face clearly said that he knew this was so much more than a snowy hookup.

Our kiss wasn't even close to sweet. He nipped at my lips like he had my skin, and it wasn't long before our tongues were intertwined, wrapping together as if we were made to be together. He groaned into my mouth and then grabbed my thighs, picked me up, wrapping my legs around his waist, and turning to the open living room.

He was so incredibly strong and after this, I was demanding that he carry me everywhere. With hardly any effort at all, he bent to his knees, and then pressed me down into the soft, furry rug. Together, we pulled my jeans down my legs, and Bridger tugged my panties off right after them. He tossed them over his shoulders, and I giggled at his disdain for my undergarments, until I saw the awe on his face.

He literally licked his lips like a kid about to walk into

a candy store with a hundred bucks. With the same careful measure he took with everything else, instead of diving in like I would have, he started slow, running his hands up and down my body to explore every inch of my skin.

His touches weren't shy. He knew exactly what he wanted and what he was doing. I couldn't help but moan when he cupped my breasts and ran his thumbs over the nipples. But he was only there long enough to tease me before his fingers were tracing the swell of my tummy and then curve of my hip. His total possession of each inch of my body left me with a rise and fall of goosebumps, and the anticipation for what he would do next.

I wanted so much to tease him right back with my own touches and words, but I could hardly do more than sigh and moan. I couldn't even come up with good dirty talk, and he hadn't even gotten between my legs yet. I was the one who was ready to beg now. I'd get him back for that when it was my turn. "Please, Bridger. Don't tease me."

"I'm barely getting started. Got to get you nice and warmed up. Just wait until I use your thighs as my own personal earmuffs."

He moved all the way down, past my thighs, and pressed little kisses and licks across each of my toes and then the tops of my feet. I'd certainly never thought ankles were an erogenous zone, but every teasing touch had me glowing hotter and hotter. "Too much more and I won't just be warm, I'm going to combust and burn the cabin down."

"I want you completely melted for me, sweetheart."

He trailed his fingers back up the outside of each leg, inching closer and closer to my core.

"If I melt anymore for you, I'm going to be a pile of goo right here on your carpet." The wicked witch of the west, or east as it was, cackled "I'm melting, I'm melting" in my head. And I might have said it out loud if he hadn't smiled, dipped his head, brushing his beard along the inside of my thigh, and pulled the fleshiest bit of my leg between his teeth, gently letting it slide between his lips. I groaned and pushed my hips up, needing him to do that exact same thing to my pussy.

"Bridger, you're going to be the death of me."

"Not until you've melted for me at least a couple dozen times." Finally, finally, finally he pressed hot kisses against my pussy lips. His tongue darted out, flicking across my clit, tasting me as if I were the most delicious treat he'd ever tasted.

He groaned or growled or both at the same time. It was a guttural moan, unable to hold himself back any longer. That kind of sound that came from a man lost in the moment. Lost in me.

His hands moved from my hips up over my stomach, caressing parts of me I didn't normally like to be touched. But with him, every part of me wanted to be caressed, worshipped. He slid his hands back down and gripped my butt in both hands, holding my pussy tight to his lips, licking and sucking and feasting on me.

The man had a tongue like a god. A really dirty, horny god.

I was going to have the best beard burn after this.

"You're fucking delicious," he whispered, as if the words weren't even for me.

I couldn't take it anymore and shoved my hands into his hair to hold him right where I needed him most. "Make me come, Bridger. Now."

Before I even finished my demand, he was on top of me, pushing my arms up over my head and into the carpet.

"I'll be inside of you when you come for me. I want to feel your cunt squeezing my cock." He said the words with a deep, almost primal force that demanded my submission, and I was powerless to deny him. I loved this little battle of wills we had going on between us. Most guys either went all squishy for a dominant woman or wouldn't play along at all. "Do you want my cock, April? Or do you want to melt for me some more?"

"Can't we do both?" I brought my knees up and wrapped my legs around his waist, locking him to me. His answer was to kiss me hard, the taste of my arousal taking me from hot to entirely ooey gooey melted in a second.

Bridger reached into his pocket. How was he still wearing his jeans? He pulled out his wallet and, in a second, had a wrapped condom ready to go. I grabbed the packet, opening it, while he finally undid his jeans and dropped them down around his knees.

Oh. Ooh. He really was the biggest linebacker in the league. Not that I had anything to compare to, but there was no way anyone else in the wide world of sports was... bigger than Bridger Kingman.

Like... if I didn't know condoms were incredibly flexible, I'd wonder if this thing was even going to fit. But I did know exactly where he was going to fit perfectly. God, I loved a big cock.

Apparently, I'd stared at his equipment for too long, because he grabbed the condom from me and rolled it down. "Don't worry, love. We'll go slow."

He must have thought my open-mouthed, slack-jawed gape was trepidation. He didn't know how wrong he was. "Don't you dare."

I loved the way he commanded what he wanted from me, but I had just as much fun telling him what to do. I wrapped my legs around his waist and twisted until he was underneath me, my weight holding him to the floor, just as his had done to me.

"I want all of you, big boy." I positioned myself and reached between us, grabbing his cock and notching the head right at my entrance. Then I moved my hips just a few inches and sank down onto his thick shaft, slowly, until he was buried as deep inside of me as I could take him.

His eyes were closed, and his head pushed down into the carpet. He was taking long, deep breaths, and I recognized his attempt at controlling himself. But I wanted him out of control. I squeezed my inner muscles rhythmically, punctuating my need for him with my body and my words at the same time. "You're mine, you are mine."

I don't know why it was so important for me to say it out loud like this again, but I needed to verbalize this claim on him. It felt like if I didn't, he'd slip away from me.

He gasped at the intensity of it all and his eyes shot open, staring up at me before they rolled back in his head.

He grabbed onto my hips and held me tight. "You want me to beg you to go faster, don't you, sweetness?"

"I definitely want to hear you beg."

I'd never been so bold and had definitely never said anything like that out loud before. Somehow, Bridger's tough exterior mixed with his sweet but boldly protective inside brought out the truest parts of me I'd hidden from even myself. "Say it, Bridger. Beg me to ride your cock until I come."

"Holy fuck that's hot." His fingers dug into the flesh at my hips. "Yes, fuck me, April. Let me watch you come apart, make yourself come on my cock."

Okay, so he was probably new to begging, because that was straight up telling me what to do. But it still hit those buttons for me. I pressed my knees into the soft rug, closed my eyes, threw my head back and resisted every impulse I had to ride him like a naughty, horny cowgirl. Instead, I slowed both his movements and mine, so that each thrust brought greater pleasure and more intensity than anything I had ever felt before.

Bridger groaned and shifted his angle slightly so that every movement massaged my inner walls in just the right way. He pulled out ever so slightly before plunging back in, each thrust slower and deeper than the last.

Our hearts pounded together in rhythm, and it felt like we were meant to be together. Like our bodies already knew we were a perfect match. His hard muscles to my soft curves, his grump to my sunshine, his careful protectiveness to my willingness to jump in with both feet. We were laying claim to every inch of each other, and nothing could be better.

Oops. I was wrong.

Just as I was about to reach down to stroke myself as I rode him, Bridger shoved my hand out of the way and slid his fingers between us, cupping my pussy, stroking my clit with his thumb.

"This pussy is mine, and so is the orgasm. Ride me, April, take my cock, but I'm the one who's making you come."

THICK THIGHS SAVE LIVES

BRIDGER

Thick thighs might save lives, but April's were about to kill me. If she didn't come in the next seven seconds, I was a dead man. Because I'd rather die than come before she did.

Sex had never in my life been this good. And I'd had a lot of sex. Being a star football player from early on, I'd never even had to chase women. But, if whatever the hell I'd been doing with every other woman before this was sex, I'd been doing it dead ass wrong.

I always made sure my partners were well taken care of, because there was nothing sexier than a woman coming on my dick when I told her too. But nothing, absolutely nothing, compared to the pure bliss of April on top of me, her cunt squeezing my cock, teetering on the edge of exploding.

"April." Her name was nothing more than a growl coming out of my soul. "Come for me. Come all over my cock, right the fuck now."

"Beg me, Bridger. Beg me to come on your cock. I need

it," she moaned out the words, whimpered her own plea. Her pussy tightened around my cock, pulsing around me.

Never in my life had I begged a woman for anything. But fuck, if that's what she needed to come, that's what I was going to give her. This goddess of a woman literally taking her pleasure from me, demanding it, had me half a breath away from falling in love with her.

I sat up, wrapped one arm around her ass so she didn't move off my lap, and shoved the other one into her hair. I gripped her pretty waves in my fist and tilted her head back, making her arch into me. With the last of my will power, I pressed my lips to her ear and growled my plea and my demand. "Please, April. Come for me now."

She ground against me one last time, and a full-body shudder rolled across her. Every muscle in her body clenched before she cried out. She grasped onto my shoulders, digging her nails into my skin as she finally exploded, her pussy clenching around me, taking me with her into the utter bliss of coming together.

I couldn't take my eyes off her, watching every pulse of her pleasure dragging the longest fucking orgasm out of me. The only thing that would have made this any better was if I'd been bare inside of her, spilling myself deep, marking her as my own.

A rush of tingles swept from my chest, spreading out in all directions. The idea of filling her with my seed, making babies with her, watching her belly grow with my children, stole my breath away.

I wanted that. And even the thought should have scared the shit out of me. But it didn't.

April's head dropped to my shoulder, and her harsh, fast breaths matched mine. I cradled her head, not willing to unthread my fingers from her hair just yet. I was cementing this scene, this feeling, her scent, everything, in my mind, because I knew it was going to be a pivotal moment in my life.

I was never letting April go.

I'd learned to trust my gut. It was how I'd chosen which school to play ball for and gone on to win every award a defensive player could while I was there. My gut told me to buy this piece of the Bear Claw, build a cabin, and start my own charity for pets rescued from natural disasters. My gut helped me become Defensive Rookie of the Year after being second draft pick and playing for the Texas Stars. It was also how I knew the Stars was no longer the place for me.

People thought I was careful with my decisions, but I just listened to my gut and followed it religiously. It had never steered me wrong.

And my gut... my heart said April was the one.

She gave a little hum of satisfaction and stretched, arching her back, pressing her tits into my chest. I lifted her head and gave her a deep kiss, claiming her mouth once again. When we broke apart, she was glassy-eyed and smiling.

"That was... I... you were..." She tipped her head to the side and blinked at me through her dark lashes. "I think you fucked my brains out. Words are hard now."

That wasn't the only thing hard. I was still inside of her, barely down from our first round, and I was getting hard for her all over again. "You were the one fucking me. But I'll be happy to return the favor."

She gave a sweet laugh that turned into a groan as I laid her back and finally pulled out of her still-tight pussy. I disposed of the condom and realized I'd have to get up to find another one. For the time being, I wasn't going anywhere.

Besides, I still wanted to have her coming on my tongue, and my fingers, and—

Bear let out a deep bark, followed by a soft, whiny cry for attention. April squealed and then giggled. "Oh, gah, that almost scared the pee out of me. I maybe forgot you had a dog... bear...enormous fuzzy ball of fur."

"You're frightened by my dog, but not me." It wasn't a question. Not once had she backed away, backed down, or anything else. It was one of the things that had me falling for her. She was a tough cookie. Even if she was a city slicker.

She reached up and booped my nose. Booped. "You're not scary. He's not either. He just startled me, because I was so into you, I forgot he existed. Bear is cute, but also, could probably eat me. I like living on the edge that way."

It took me a minute to recover from the nose booping before I could respond. "I'm not scary?"

Honestly, when was the last time I'd met anyone who wasn't a little bit scared of me? Came with the territory of being six-five and almost three hundred pounds of mostly muscle. Not to mention being named the football league's meanest player.

"Maybe if I was a quarterback you were sacking. You'd probably scare the bejeesus out of me."

I wanted to make a joke about sacking her. But I was a bit too stunned.

"You know who I am?" She was from Texas, and I had been playing ball there for the last four years. It made sense that she knew I was. My brain screamed 'ball bunny' but my gut said she was something so much more.

"Yeah. I grew up in a bit of a sports family." She smiled just a little shyly, but I didn't think it was over my fame, but because she was talking about her family. That had me curious. "My dad's been following your career since you played at Nebraska. No one else has ever won the Bronko Nagurski Trophy, the Chuck Bednarik Award, the Lombardi Award, the Outland Trophy, and AP's Football Player of the Year, like you did."

Okay, normal city slicker women didn't even know the difference between offensive and defensive players, much less the names of the college football awards. "Uh, who's your dad, April?"

"Oh, yeah, umm, he's Hunter De la Reine."

Oh shit. Only sports' most powerful, well-known agent. Which made April his protege daughter. "Huh. I guess, well, I know who you are now too."

She shrugged and tried to pull away, but I didn't let her. I held her tight and cupped her chin. "Doesn't change anything, sweetheart. So I'm famous, and you're rich and famous. I still want to fuck your brains out. And not because of your father or anything else."

She finally met my eyes, and there was relief and something else I was hoping for shining in them. "Umm, I know what kind of contract you have. You're rich too."

"And what if I told you, I was ready to throw it all

away? Would you care?" I already knew the answer. April had told her old man to fuck off when he'd tried to corner her into taking over his agency when he retired. She understood the merit of following your own dreams instead of someone else's.

"No." She waggled one eyebrow at my lower half. "It'd be a shame never to see your ass in those tight football pants ever again, but I'd never tell anyone not to be who and what they want for themselves. Plenty of people have thought they could do that to me, and it stinks."

"Okay then. If that part is out of the way, we can spend the rest of this storm getting to know each other. And I very much want to know everything about you."

"You just want to get in my pants again." She laughed, but I recognized a test when I saw one.

That was fine. Just because I'd fallen head over heels in three seconds flat, didn't mean she had.

"I do. But I want a lot more from you. There's something special between us, and it's not just the sex. I like you. A lot." I knew better than to scare her away by saying anything more than that. If it took me the rest of my life, I was going to convince this girl to marry me and have my babies. Lots and lots of babies.

She didn't immediately respond to that, and I was going to give her a minute to process what I was saying.

Fuck, I hoped she wanted kids. I didn't even realize I wanted any until I imagined little blue-eyed mini versions of April running around with a whole herd of big, fluffy dogs.

Better start with the dogs. I turned back toward the kitchen, looking for Bear. He'd probably curled back up by the water heater. "Bear, come here boy. Come have a proper intro to our guest, buddy."

No fluffy head or wagging tail popped out. Weird. Where did he go? "Bear?"

A big snuffle and groan like he was put upon that I was calling him sounded from behind April. He was laying on her other side, not three feet from the fireplace, calm and as comfy as could be. I gently stroked him in that soft spot between his eyes. "When did you sneak over there, you big fluffball?"

Spoke to how completely focused on April I was and my imagining of our future life together. "I think I'm not the only one who likes you. He's never been this close to the fireplace in his life. He's scared of it."

"I like him too." She ran her fingers over his head and gave him a scritch behind his ear. "Why is he scared of the fireplace? He seems pretty fine with it now."

"He was caught up in a forest fire here in Colorado when he was a puppy. We have them pretty much every summer. Poor guy was a wreck. Patches of fur burned away, smoke inhalation."

"You rescued him?" She looked up at me like I was some kind of knight in shining armor. I was just a guy with a soft spot for animals. Especially ones in need.

"Yeah. He stays with my folks up here during the season." Wouldn't be fair to have him down in Texas when I'm on the road all the time. But if I moved back to Colorado, he'd be by my side a lot more than just my bye-weeks. "I just picked him up from them this morning. Gotta have my guy by my side for the big shindig this weekend."

"Shindig?" Both April and Bear gave me that what-are-you-talking-about head tilt. These two were made for each other.

"Yeah. Our holiday Cause for Paws." We did fundraising like this a couple of times a year, but the holiday one always brought in the most money. Probably because I made a bunch of professional athletes donate time or money or prizes. Being scary had its advantages. "There's a 5K where everyone brings their dogs, then we do a big cookout and a party over at the ski resort. There's a silent auction, and we raise a bunch of money for local shelters and make funds available specially to take care of pets that have been affected by natural disasters."

"That's... very cool. But won't you have to cancel?" She waved an arm at the window.

"This is Bear Claw Valley, doll. We love a little snow." The ski resort on the other side of the hill was likely doing a happy dance for all the fresh powder they were getting.

"Little?" She shook her head at me, and Bear gave a little woof in solidarity.

"What? Everything is little compared to me." Except April. She and I fit together exactly right.

"You got me there." She winked and let out a chuckle that made my heart do flips in my chest. "I guess everything is small when you're as big as a bear."

"You'll go with me to the Cause for Paws stuff tomorrow, won't you?"

"I'll have to cheer you and Bear on from the finish line of the 5K, because, you know, fancy high-heeled boots.

But yeah, it all sounds like fun, and I'm always down for a good cause."

Here goes nothing... or everything. "And after that?"

She turned in my arms, and this time she was the one who pushed her hands into my hair. "I don't know, but," she brushed her lips across mine, pulling away too fast to let me kiss her as I wanted, "I like you, too, Bridger. Even if you're the absolute worst at begging."

I was ready to beg her to stay with me forever. "I think it's probably going to take a long time for you to teach me that particular skill, sweetheart."

"Then you'd better hope it keeps snowing. Too bad we didn't bring my suitcase. I'm fairly sure I packed my fuzzy handcuffs. Oh, wait. Do you have any duct tape?"

EPILOGUE: CAUSE FOR PAWS

APRIL

One year later~

"Does it ever not snow for Cause for Paws?" I clapped my hands together, waiting for Bridger to open the cabin door.

Bear was still running circles in the fluffy stuff and trying to eat the snowflakes. At least this year it wasn't a whole ass blizzard. But this was the coldest I'd been since we'd both made the move to Denver. Who knew Colorado had three-hundred days of sunshine a year?

Bear Claw Valley on the other hand, once again had fresh snow. Good for skiing. Sucky for cute boots. And no, I was never giving up my cute ass boots.

"Not that I can ever remember." He gave the door a good shake, and it still didn't budge.

The 5k and the party at the ski resort had been the most successful fundraiser for the charity in its entire history. Partly because I was an excellent event planner, and partly because half of Colorado had shown up. I'd always thought Texans made sports a priority, but Denver? Man, that was a sports-crazy town if I ever lived in one.

They loved that a hometown boy was back. The Mustangs had made him an offer even his shitty agent couldn't refuse. But Bridger had. And now he was the defense coach for the Denver State Dragons college football team. Next year, he'd be their head coach.

He loved it. I loved seeing him so happy. He was amazing with the kids. Someday soon he was going to be an amazing dad. But he didn't know that yet.

We didn't spend as much time here as I would like, but I treasured every moment when we did. Most of my days were spent in Denver, pursuing my dreams and forging my own path, doing something I really felt made a difference this time.

I'd started a non-profit to promote body positivity and inclusivity in the fashion world, helping young models navigate the industry and empowering them to challenge the status quo. Denver wasn't the most body positive town, and I found myself fighting fatphobia in small ways and big nearly every day. Especially in the media.

It was challenging work, but incredibly fulfilling. But there were days I wanted to crawl into a hole when one too many concerned trolls told me to eat a salad. Bridger was always there to support me, to listen when I needed to vent, to celebrate my victories, and tell the assholes to eat a bag of dicks.

We were a team, in every sense of the word.

Bridger smirked at me, winking. "Sweetheart, could you come here and help me give this stubborn door a good shove?"

Knowing full well he could have easily manhandled that door open himself, I arched an eyebrow but went along with it anyway. Mustering my strength, we both pushed on the count of three. The door swung open easily, as if it had never been stuck in the first place. I sent Bridger a suspicious glance, but he just shrugged, his eyes twinkling with mischief.

As I stepped inside the warm cabin, I was taken with what I saw. It was aglow with the soft, romantic flicker of dozens of candles, their light dancing on the wooden walls and ceiling, making the whole place feel like a dream. The rough-around-the-edges cabin we knew so well had been transformed into an intimate sanctuary for just the two of us.

Bridger whistled for Bear, shut the door behind him, and pulled me into our perfectly warm and cozy sanctuary. He wrapped me into a bear hug, our bodies perfectly in sync. I could feel his heart racing in his chest. It matched the rhythm of my own.

"April De la Reine," he started, his voice shaking slightly with a mix of nervousness and excitement, which was totally out of character for the Bridger I knew and loved. He was all confidence and bravado all the time. Why was he saying my full name? What in the world could be wrong?

He brushed his lips across mine and gah, wasn't I being silly. There was nothing wrong, and everything was right. He was just flirting and trying to get into my pants. He didn't have to try this hard. I wasn't even wearing any panties tonight. They'd ruin the line of the tight leggings I was wearing.

Bridger went down on one knee and patted his leg for Bear to come over. Our big ball of fluff spun in a circle and sat down, still wagging his tail. I think he knew what was going on too. Bridger pulled out a small pouch, which I hadn't noticed in all the fur, that was attached to Bear's collar. He turned it upside down, and a small box dropped into his hand. My breath hitched as I looked at him, my eyes wide with surprise.

"You know I'm not one to beg. I mean, who could resist all this?" He gestured at his broad chest and muscled arms. His eyes twinkled in the candlelight, his grin boyishly charming.

I was going all swoony and gooey inside. I wanted to scream yes, yes, yes. But I bit my lip to give him the chance to play out his scene and actually pop the question.

"But for you," he opened the box to reveal a ridiculously huge, sparkling diamond ring, "I'd beg every single day. So, April, will you please be my wife?"

Caught in the golden candlelight, his hope-filled eyes and the immense love I felt for this man, I had only one answer. "Yes," I whispered, my voice quivering with emotion. "Yes, Bridger. I will."

I bent and grabbed his face, loving the rough feeling of his beard, and kissed him and kissed him and kissed him. Then, nudging him with a cheeky smile, I added, "And for the record, you look really good on your knees for me, big boy."

Need more of the Cocky Kingmans?

**Grab *The C*ck Down the Block*,
book one in this fun sports romance series!**

ANTS IN SANTA'S PANTS

LET IT SNOW!

Levi's been looking forward to the Kingman family game night holiday edition. Instead he's stuck in a snowstorm, when the power goes out, with only a faux bearskin rug and the cutest ever rental cabin hostess dressed only in her holiday jammies to keep him warm. Yeah, this Christmas there's more than a little anticipation in this Santa's pants.

LEVI

Snow. I fucking hate snow.

Unless of course I'm lying in front of a roaring fire with a hot, naked woman under me with the snow coming down while we do all kinds of things to keep each other warm.

That was not the case. I was in a tiny compact car I barely fit into, driving through a snowpacolypse.

But I guess I'd better get used to the cold and snow if I was moving to Denver. I'd been in Florida for a long damn time, and Texas before that, so it had been a while since I'd suffered through the wet, white fluff. I certainly didn't give a damn about a white Christmas.

The only thing that would get me to drive through a fucking blizzard on Christmas Eve was the promise of a holiday style Kingman Family Game Night. I'd been anticipating this reunion with my giant swath of cousins more than a kid waiting up for Santa Claus. There was nothing comparable to their big, boisterous family get togethers. They made everyone feel like they belonged.

It had been years since the me and my mom had done Christmas with my uncle and his brood of eight. But those were some of my favorite childhood memories and being back in the fold was what made this move worth it.

People didn't call us Kingman's the American Royalty of football for nothing. My agent had worked hard to get me traded to the Mustangs because Kingman boys were the best in the biz and I wanted to play with more of the best. But that could all wait until the new year. Tonight, I was taking each and every one of my rough and rowdy cousins down in the annual Christmas charades. Well, everyone but Jules. She was a cute kid, but a ruthless judge when it came to game night with the family.

Her I was buttering up with every teen magazine they had at both Miami international airport and DIA. That is if I ever actually made it to Leadville. The snow had been gently falling like a pretty Christmas card when I'd landed in Denver. Three hours into my two and a half hour drive up the mountain and it was a full-on blizzard. I was already anxiously creeping along in zero visibility on the mountain road at all of seventeen miles an hour.

If I didn't find this little Airbnb cabin I'd rented in the next few minutes I was begging for a corner and a pillow on the floor of the Kingman's place. Didn't matter if every available bed, couch and hammock was already claimed or that even as kids they all snored like chainsaws and I probably wouldn't get a wink of sleep, and I'd end up with a crick in the neck, not to mention a sore back.

Okay, maybe I didn't want to sleepover, which is why I'd rented a room in someone else's home last minute. It was only for a couple of nights and then I could head back down the mountain to Denver and stay at the Monaco or the Four Seasons for Go Red for Women Fun-raiser and New Year's. Then I'd hunt for a more permanent place to live.

If I didn't turn into a popsicle first. How did Coloradans do this on a regular basis?

Finally the warm light of electricity shined through the snow and I squinted at the outline of what had to be the cabin up ahead. It was either that or I'd already died of hypothermia and that was the light at the end of the tunnel.

I pulled up directly in front of the door, grabbed my bag with the required Santa suit for game night in it, and bolted up the couple of stairs to the porch, eyeballing the huge drifts of snow on the roof and trees. I probably should have gone straight to the Kingman's and face the punishment of showing up in street clothes instead of the Christmas uniform. Too late now.

The wind blew so hard the trees surrounding the cabin creaked and groaned, swaying and shaking. They looked as if they could come crashing down at any moment. I knocked and then knocked again.

Where was the owner to let me in? There was no lock box on the door or a keypad entry and there hadn't been any messages saying I needed to let myself in so I knocked again, a lot harder this time. A face appeared at the window, but I couldn't make out the features through the frost, blowing snow, and my extreme shivers.

Thank fuck someone was home, because I was about to break in. The door swung open and a few clumps of snow from the precarious drifts on the roof dropped down onto my shoulders.

The cutest Christmas elf crossed with a dust bunny I'd ever met stood in the threshold in a fuzzy gray onesie covered in repeating Rudolph the Red-Nosed reindeer print, a smear of black ash across one cheek, and hair that might have recently been on fire. She brandished a fire poker as a makeshift weapon.

She looked at me, glanced out into the storm behind me, and then raised one eyebrow. "What in sweet baby Awkwafina are you doing out in this blizzard?"

Trying to not be in it. "Are you O. Live? I reserved the room in your house for two nights."

Not that the entire cabin was much bigger than Cheeze-it. Maybe there was a secret room of requirements that appeared when a guest showed up. Otherwise, dust bunny and I were getting cozy. Which was something I wouldn't mind one bit. She was cute AF. Maybe after the Kingman Christmas Eve game night.

She snort laughed and dropped her weapon to her side. "Oh, that makes way more sense than you being a serial killer who only murders lonely spinsters in blizzard conditions on Christmas. I'm Olive. You must be Levi Kingman. I didn't think you were still coming."

The way her highly active imagination matched her adorably chaotic appearance had my attention in all the most fun ways. "Can I come in, please?"

"Oh geez, sorry. Yes, of course." The second the words were out of her mouth, her eyes went wide and she grabbed the front of my shirt. The cracking wood sound of a tree falling kaboomed as loud as a bomb going off behind me.

"Look out." She yanked hard, sending us both tumbling into the cabin, with an avalanche of snow from the roof and tree branches chasing us through the door. I landed right on top of her, face to boobs. If my feet weren't buried in ice, I'd take the time to peruse her luscious delights. She was soft in all the places I was hard and I was getting harder by the second.

I couldn't continue to be a running back if my feet got frostbite and had to be amputated though. I wrapped my arms around her, twisted and rolled, pulling my lower half out of the pile of snow and looked back to assess the damage. More snow and debris dumped down and covered the entirety of the front door, drifting into the cabin.

Through the window, I saw the thick tree trunk askew against the cabin and compacting more snow along the front of the little house. But that was it. I couldn't see outside at all. I didn't know if this was a full-on mountain sized avalanche, or just her front yard, but either way, I could be dead right now. "I think you just saved my life."

She was breathing fast and her pupils were blown. That fight or flight response had definitely been triggered. Fuck, why was that so damn hot? Without even thinking, I lifted my head up and pressed my lips to hers.

She should have slapped me. Instead she kissed me back.

I loved me some anticipation, but there was something to be said for skipping to the good part.

OLIVE

I hadn't asked Santa for anything since I was seven years old and gotten a pair of socks from my new foster family instead of the puppy I knew my parents would have gotten for me. But if I was going to ask for anything, it would definitely be a six-foot-six wall of muscles, and sex appeal kissing me like it was the end of the world.

He tasted like mint, no cinnamon, and temptation.

I'm fairly sure I wasn't supposed to sleep with the people who rented out my spare room, and if the two of us kept rolling around on the floor like this, I was going to invite a stranger right into my bed. It had been far too long since I'd even had another person touch me, much less stick their tongue down my throat in ways that had me wanting so much more.

Normally my brain zipped from one thought to the next and the next and the next, and aside from wondering what brand of toothpaste Levi used, kissing him was the most in the moment I'd felt in years. They should definitely bottle his kisses and sell them as ADHD medication.

Or maybe it was simply the fact that I was in actual physical contact with another person that had me laser focused. Did I know I was starved for human touch? Sure, I did. Wasn't much I could do about it when the only people I saw on a regular basis were on my computer screen. Zoom room sexy times with the head of the temp firm I worked for was definitely not on my Christmas wish list. Hell, it wasn't even on my Amazon wish list.

Levi rolled us again so that he was over me, and I will admit that if he'd stripped me out of my cozy pjs and railed me on the cold wood floor of my aunt's disaster of a cabin, I would not have said no. Unfortunately, instead of fulfilling that fantasy, he broke the kiss.

He licked his lips and his eyes flashed from my eyes to my lips and back again in a way that had me wondering if he was about to suggest we move this to a bed. "This is the best Christmas gift I've gotten in years, but I think we'd better see if we can dig the snow and tree branches out of your front door."

"Oh, umm, yeah." I glanced away, knowing I was now turning every shade of pink, red, and fuchsia. "Sorry about that. Guess the excitement got to me."

"Oh, don't apologize. If there wasn't a wall of snow ready to come tumbling down on us, and I didn't have a family Christmas party to get to, I wouldn't have stopped until you wanted me too." His smile gave me flutters in my lower belly. He was a serious flirt and I shouldn't swoon for that, but I was. Like a thousand percent.

He jumped up, reached a hand down to me and pulled

me up to my feet too. Even that perfunctory touch gave me the warm and fuzzies. He pushed some of the snow that had been thrown into the doorway around with his tennis shoes. Where was this boy's coat and boots?

I'd moved here from Florida when long-lost-didn't-know-she-existed Aunt Verbena left me the cabin three months ago, but even I knew I needed a coat in winter in the mountains. Duh. "You're gonna catch your death of the cold. Maybe we should just try to shut the door and wait out the storm."

"No can do, bunny. I've got a family shindig to get to." He poked five fingers into the wall of snow and grabbed a fistful of icy slush. "You got a back door to this place?"

"No, but there's a window in the guest room. Maybe you can crawl out. But I don't think you should be going back out into this storm."

"Let's get this door shut so the blizzard stays outside and then I'll change and head over to my family's. If we get you all snugged up here, I can bring them back in the morning and clear out your front porch for you." He kicked more snow to the side and got the door about three quarters the way closed before it got caught up on the drift of snow blocking the who entryway.

I grabbed the broom and dustpan I'd been using to clean, and the tiny shovel for the fireplace ashes. It's all I had to work with since the actual snow shovel was leaning against the front of the house buried in snow somewhere. We scraped and swept and I dumped snow into the sink to get rid of it until we finally got enough cleared away to get the door to close.

Levi let out a long puff of air and shook his hands,

then rubbed them together and blew warm breath on them. "Okay. Let's see about that bedroom window."

I pointed him toward the guest room. I hadn't been able to get the window to budge since there was about seventeen layers of paint sealing it shut. I'd barely gotten the room cleaned up and looking livable when his reservation had come in yesterday.

Another big boom, followed by a crash and breaking glass sounded from the bedroom as if I'd conjured it up with my finger as a magic wand.

"That was the window in question, wasn't it?"

"Yes." I squeaked. I rushed over and yanked the door to the room open, gasped and then shut it. "Oh no. No, no, no, no."

"What?" Levi put his hand over mine and reopened the door. "Shit."

"That's pretty much what I said." Another tree had blown down in the storm and was currently sticking straight through not only the window, but the roof and a whole new hole in the wall.

He gawked at the disaster zone and then took my cue and shut the door. "Maybe we can get out the window in your room?"

"That was my room until you rented it. I'm fresh out of rooms and windows. And doors."

"Then you're coming with me to the Kingman's. We'll just have to dig our way out." He pulled his cell phone from his pocket and held it up. I already knew he didn't have any bars. I never got a signal out here either, which is why I'd gotten the best satellite internet I could afford.

"Try the Wi-Fi."

He flipped to the settings, found Verbena Cabin 5.0 which of course was the only network available, and Facetimed someone in his contacts called QB. A man who looked just slightly older than Levi, but bore a striking resemblance answered wearing a Santa hat. "Levi, dude. Did you find a place in town or are you stuck at camp DIA?"

"Chris, hey. No, I made it to my Airbnb, but we're snowed--" Before he could finish his sentence, the lights in the whole cabin went out and his call dropped. No power, no internet.

No power, no heat.

We were going to die. I gave Levi a long up and down look. How long could we keep each other warm with only our body heat?

LEVI

"Well, shit." This was just not the way I expected my Christmas Eve to go. Why the hell was the universe conspiring against me going to a good old family party? I glanced over at Olive with only the light from my phone illuminating the room. Her eyes flicked around and then she stared up at me like I was supposed to be her saving grace in all this mess.

The thing was, I wanted to be. So maybe the universe wasn't conspiring against me, but for me. For me and her. Because there was definitely something out there working really hard to get the two of us alone together.

"I don't suppose you have a backup generator in your bag, do you?" She blurted that out and smiled, but it was not a great attempt at covering up her fear.

"Nope. Just a Santa suit and some teeny bopper magazines. Oh, and a half eaten Toblerone."

"I love those things."

"Santa suits or teeny bopper magazines?" She gave me

a more genuine smile and while we were still in trouble here, that elevated level of tension dropped. We were in this together whether we liked it or not, and I liked it, a lot.

Not the missing Christmas, but if I had to, I had a feeling this slightly wacky woman was the one person that would make a disastrous night feel just right. Especially if we had to snuggle to keep warm. Was that my heart skipping a beat?

Yes, yes it was. I moved closer, fully intending on starting to share body heat sooner rather than later. "We'd better do something about not freezing to death."

"I was trying to figure out how to get a fire going in the fireplace when you got here."

Oh, that's what the ashes and burned hair was all about. "If you've also got a bear skin rug for us to lay on in front of it. I'm game."

Olive went from that slightly worried look to absolutely horrified. "Umm, I'm not in the habit of keeping dead animal remains in my house. I'll have you know I donate to that sad puppy and kitty commercial every time it comes on."

I held up my free hand. "Okay, okay. No dead animals. That's fine. I only meant I wouldn't mind getting cozy in front of the fire with you."

"With me?" She looked around the cabin. "Sorry, that probably made me sound like a twit. Sometimes my mouth doesn't keep up with my brain and you wouldn't be the first person to accuse me of saying weird shit."

"I kinda like your mouth." I wanted to kiss her again,

right here, right now. Who cared if it was already cold in here, I knew how to warm us both up.

She grinned again, and touched her lips. "I liked yours too. Now quit flirting with me and help me figure out how to build a fire. It's not as easy as it looks in movies."

"You're in luck." And I was hoping to get lucky. "I was a boy scout. Assuming you've got matches and wood, we'll get a nice fire going and then we'll have our own Christmas party."

A naked one if I had my way.

I used the flashlight on my phone to light our path, which was all of ten steps, over to the fireplace where there was a stack of logs, old ashes, and whole pile of used wooden matches. She didn't have any tinder or kindling whatsoever, just a mess and a half.

We both knelt in front of the fireplace and I worked on re-arranging the logs into a teepee that would actually burn instead of her Tetris style stack.

She grabbed the box of matches and handed them over. "I'm not much for celebrating the holidays."

Huh. I fricking loved every minute from Labor Day all the way to New Years. The holidays and football went hand in hand. What wasn't there to like? I shook the box and a lone match rattled around. When I slid it open, yep, sure enough, one single match.

"When you said you were giving me your room, I figured you were going to your family's for the night or something." I got up and grabbed my bag. Jules's magazines were going to have to be sacrificed to Hephaestus.

"Oh. No. I don't have any family." She set that bomb off so matter of factly, I almost missed it.

"Wait. What? No family?" That explained not liking the holiday season. It had just been me and my mom most of the time growing up, but she always made sure my friends and teammates were welcome for every celebration big or small and made everyone feel like family. I'd dragged half the offensive line home for Winter break more than once. "Friends then?"

I kept my tone to casual conversation mode, pretending it didn't hurt my heart that she appeared to be all alone. I ripped pages out of Teen Beat and shredded some, twisted others into little paper logs, and then shoved the into a big pile in the center of our logs. Mixed with the leftover match remnants and a few strips of bark, and I did my pack leader proud.

Olive still hadn't answered my question. I didn't like that. Not because I thought I deserved an answer or anything, but because her silence was far too telling. As soon as this fire was lit, I was wrapping her in my arms and she and I were becoming friends. Maybe even with benefits.

I sent a little prayer out to the universe to let this be the best one match fire that ever was, and struck the thing against the side of the box. It ignited, and burned steady as I cupped my hand around it and leaned into the fireplace. The magazine shreds were not the best tinder and that flame got much closer to my fingers than I wanted before they finally took.

It took me a couple of long, slow puff of air to get real flames licking at the logs, but finally they took. It was a Christmas miracle. Rock the fuck on. I turned to high five

Olive, but she was staring into the fireplace without any cheer in her eyes.

"Umm." She stared into the first flickering flames a little longer than was comfortable. "I didn't move here that long ago, and I've mostly been working and trying to fix up the cabin. I haven't really prioritized making friends here."

I sat on the floor next to her. "I just moved here too and aside from my uncle and cousins, I don't know anyone either. So why don't you and I be each other's first pal in Colorado? That way we're both spending Christmas with a friend."

She gave me a cute smirk smile. "You're weird."

I snort laughed. Like actually snorted. I was the least weird person I knew, and Olive was a deliciously odd duck. "Yep. That's me. Now, we might be stuck here, but that doesn't mean we can't have a Christmas party of our own. What kind of reindeer games shall we play?"

"Don't you do like presents and sing carols or something? Reindeer games aren't a real thing."

"Uh, yeah they are. Where do you think the lyrics to the song came from? My favorite part of Christmas is kicking everyone else's butt at Christmas charades."

The logs crackled as the blaze got going and the light and warmth cast Olive in the most beautiful light. She may look like a wreck, but she was also an angel. "That's not a thing."

I scooted closer, not because I was cold, but just to be nearer to her. "Oh, I assure you it is. Along with Christmas Pictionary, Christmas Mad-Libs, Christmas

Scrabble, and pin the tail on Rudolph. My family is extremely competitive."

"What does the winner get?"

There was a long-standing tradition of the game night winners getting to lay claim to a really obnoxious homemade trophy. But since said trophy was safe and sound at the Kingman cabin, we'd need a different prize.

I had just the thing. "A Christmas kiss, of course."

OLIVE

*L*evi was maybe the sweetest tough guy I'd ever met. I'd been right on the verge of going completely melancholy and he wasn't having any of it. I probably would have ignored the holiday all together if he hadn't come along. It's what I did most of the time anyway.

But his enthusiasm and completely unbothered attitude about the storm, the state of disrepair of my aunt's cabin, and the fact that we were completely snowed in and stuck here until who knows when was like a balm to my overly freaking out mind.

"A kiss huh. So your family has kissing cousins?"

He screwed up his face and laughed. "No. No, no, no. We have a silly gold trophy. But since we don't have it, I figured a kiss was the next best prize."

His eyes did that thing where he stared at my mouth again, and I couldn't help but lick my lips. I wanted to kiss Levi again.

He eyeballed the tiny mid-century modern couch and

then me. "If you'd planned to give up your room for me, where exactly were you planning to sleep?"

I pointed to the ladder that led to the tiny loft above the kitchen. "I've got a sleeping bag and one of those camping pads up there."

I hadn't really thought anyone would actually take me up on my last-minute room rental listing. I didn't even know why I'd placed it. There wasn't really room for two people to have their own space here. Maybe I was tired of being out here all alone.

Maybe I was tired of feeling alone.

Maybe I was going to do something about that right here, right now. "I guess we'll have to share it for the night."

Levi's eyes sparkled in the firelight and he leaned in. "I guess we will."

Our lips met again, and this time, the kiss wasn't frantic, or adrenaline fueled, but soft, sweet, and full of anticipation. He slid his mouth over mine, teasing me with the temptation of what was to come. "I think I like this game even better than Christmas charades."

"Me too." His tongue darted out and licked along the corner of my mouth. He groaned as if I tasted like his favorite dessert.

I opened for him, wanting to invite him to make the kiss deeper, and then remembered that I was the one who decided I wanted more. So instead of waiting for his move, I pushed my way into his mouth. I'd never done anything so bold in my life and it had my insides tingling and my outsides heating up.

I'd always felt too awkward and weird to initiate

anything with my past boyfriends. But going for what I wanted was turning out to be way more satisfying already.

He grinned up at me and hands snaked up my back and into my hair. "Olive, I know I said the prize was a kiss, but we don't have to do anything more."

"We haven't even played your reindeer games yet, and I definitely want more." I kissed him again and got another soft, husky groan. I always thought women were the only ones who made all the sounds, but I was thoroughly enjoying his. I couldn't wait to wring even more out of him.

Levi wrapped his arms around me and pulled me into his lap. I wanted more of this heady being in charge feeling. I rearranged our positions so that I straddled his thighs and our torsos were even. In an instant my hot skin went icy cold. I squealed and jumped away.

"Have you been sitting here in those icy cold, wet jeans this whole time?" We'd been so busy escaping avalanches of snow and trees that I hadn't realized he'd gotten soaked.

"Guess I'd better take them off, huh?"

"Yes, and get warm."

"I don't think the fire is going to be enough. You'd better get undressed too and--"

I unzipped my fuzzy pajamas and dropped them to the floor. Impulse control was never one of my strong suits. Levi apparently forgot how to talk because he cut off mid-sentence with his mouth just hanging open.

That wasn't the first time someone went mute when I did something they didn't expect, but it was the only time

I'd made someone dumbstruck because I was butt naked. The difference this time was the look on Levi's face. It wasn't that usual you're-so-weird-I-don't-know-how-to-react blank stare. Nope. He looked more like a kid on Christmas morning.

"Let me help you get out of your clothes and get warm." I lifted the hem of his t-shirt and he snagged it from me, flipping it over his head in a second and tossing it over his shoulder.

"I always got told growing up that I had ants in my pants because I couldn't wait for everyone else around me to do or say or think at the speed I was going. You're the first person I've ever met who not only keeps up, but is running circles around me. I fucking love it."

Huh. Brain going too fast. Yeah, that's exactly what I felt like all the damn time. I reached for the button on his jeans. "What if I told you I like ants?"

"Of course you do." Together we peeled his wet clothes off of his legs and he sighed in relief. His skin was cold to the touch and I worried that getting lost in the moment was going to do more damage than good.

I draped his jeans across the back of a chair and propped it on the side of the fireplace, and then I opened up the big wooden chest that served as a coffee table. There was about a dozen handmade quilts inside that I had no idea what I'd ever do with.

They were soft and smelled of cedar and were going to make the best nest right here in front of the fireplace. I hauled them out and giggled at what I found underneath. At the bottom of the chest was a vacuum sealed bag labeled: faux bear skin rug. Two googly eyes of a squarshed polar bear looked up at me.

Levi came over and looked into the chest. "Yes. Bear skin rug. Perfect."

He grabbed it out, unzipped the seal and pulled the folded rug out. It was only about half as tall as he was, but with each passing moment exposed to the air once again, it got fluffier. He laid it down on the wooden floor, flopped down on it, and crooked his finger at me. "Come over here with those blankets and warm me up."

LEVI

I'm not sure how or when, but I'd fallen for Olive. No, that wasn't true. I knew it was the first moment. My soul recognized hers right away. She was cute, and adorable, and chaotic, and exactly what I needed in my life. Because without even hearing a word out of her mouth, something deep inside of me knew that she saw me.

The real me.

Not the star football player, not the player accused of having a new girl on his arm every weekend, and not the guy who drove everyone crazy when I acted first and thought second.

She saw the man who, despite having a big important family who I loved, needed someone of my very own to belong to, and someone who belonged to me.

That was some deep fucking thoughts and feelings for someone I'd known only a few hours. Some might think I was batshit crazy, but somehow I knew Olive wouldn't.

Why wait when it was so god damned clear that we were made for each other.

Now was exactly the right time to show her how I felt.

I ripped the faux bearskin rug out of its shrink wrap and spread it out in front of the fireplace. It had been cut to vaguely resemble the outline of a polar bear, mounted on some kind of soft felt-like backing where claws had been drawn on.

"It's the offset googly eyes that do it for me," I said with a chuckle.

Olive tossed a blanket over the bear's face. "Yeah, no. I don't want him watching us."

I wrapped my hands around her waist and pulled her down to the carpet with me so we were kneeling, face to face, chest to chest, hips to hips. Even though I was twice her size, we fit together so perfectly.

"Exhibitionism not your kink?" I was teasing, but Olive gasped and her eyes flicked from side to side. It was entirely amusing to watch her process that. It took her a bit longer, because I distracted her by skimming my hands along the soft curve of her hip, up to the dip in her waist, and over to the swell of her breasts.

She leaned into my and traced a finger down my chest, exploring my body right back. "Is it one of yours?"

"Never thought about it. We can investigate that later if you want." I bent and pressed my lips to her jaw and then her collarbone. "But I will tell you what one of mine is."

"Ooh. Is this the I'll show you mine if you show me yours reindeer game?" She threaded her hands into my hair and showed me exactly where she wanted me to kiss her. There was a particular spot below her ear that made her gasp in the most delicious way.

"Yes. Absolutely." I pushed her hair aside and found the tiniest tattoo from behind her ear and into her hairline. Little black ants with tiny antennas marching in a crooked line into her hairline. I licked each and every one.

She shivered and leaned into me. "Fun. I think I'd like to try Japanese Shibari, sensory play, and double penetration with dildos."

My brain detonated and it took a minute for the mushroom cloud of that erotic image explosion to settle. "I was just going to say that my kink is a pretty woman who know what they want, but that sounds fun too. I think you win this round."

I fucking loved that I never knew what she was going to do or what was coming out of her mouth. That so rarely happened to me and it was more exciting than any deliberate games of anticipation I'd ever played in bed before. She would keep me on my toes, and I never wanted to let that feeling go.

The way she utterly leaned into the pandemonium of this entire night loosened the hold I had on myself. I'd spent my whole life either being told to slow down and think about what I was doing or making sure others didn't think I was jumping into something I wasn't prepared for.

Nothing could have prepared me for Olive and that was everything I'd ever wanted and never been allowed to indulge in. And now I was going to indulge in her.

Without needing to think about it or wonder if she would be okay with my actions, I reached down and grabbed her behind the knees and lifted her up to lay her across the rug in exactly the position I wanted. She squealed and giggled, but when I climbed over her and spread her knees with mine, she waggled her eyebrows at me.

"What's this game called?"

"The how many orgasms can I give Olive before her eyes roll back in her head game." I dropped a kiss to her belly, then to her right thigh, and then to her pussy. Her scent shot straight to my cock and my first wet taste of her had me so close to coming I had to fist the rug in my hands to hold myself back. But nothing was stopping me from licking her to at least two of three climaxes.

I found her clit with my tongue and swirled around and around, half fucking the floor at the same time, wanting so badly to be inside of her, but needing to make sure she came first and often before I even considered my own pleasure.

Olive pushed her hands into my hair and thrust her hips forward, reaching for more from me. "This is about to be my favorite reindeer game."

Oh, fuck yeah. She was on the verge of coming and I'd barely gotten to the good part. With so many of my past partners, I would draw this out by slowing down and teasing, but that wasn't what either of us wanted. And thank God.

I doubled down and rapidly flicked my tongue over her clit as fast as I could, and pushed two fingers inside, crooking them until I found just the right spot.

"Oh, Santa, yes, yes, yes." Olive bucked against my mouth and I felt the rhythmic pulse of her orgasm squeezing my fingers. I was adding a smidge of daddy kink to her list for calling me Santa.

When her body went limp, I crawled back over her and nuzzled my way back to those little ant tattoos behind her ear. She wrapped her arms around my neck until her rapid breathing finally slowed. Then she whispered, "One."

"One?" I wanted to hear her say I'd given her a great fucking orgasm.

She gave me a shove, and pushed me away, but so that she could get on top. "Game over. It took one orgasm for you to make my eyes roll back in my head."

I pressed my hands on either side of her hips and rocked my cock against the apex of her legs. "That was just the first round of the game. Now I have to see if I can beat my best score and I'll have you know I'm very competitive."

OLIVE

Where had Levi been my whole life? I always was a love at first sight kind of girl. It took me all of forty-seven seconds to fall in love with him, and with most guys, that would have freaked them out. Not Levi.

I was lying in his arms after I'd ridden him like a naughty cowgirl for the third time tonight. He'd gotten up to put another log on the fire a few times and each time I'd wanted to tell him I loved him and instead ended up jumping his bones. Those six-bazillion pack abs were just so distracting.

But now that the blizzard was calming the hell down, and the sun was peeking in through the trees I couldn't hold it in for another moment. "Levi?"

He ran his fingers through my hair, petting and caressing me. "Yeah, bunny?"

"I--" Had more feelings than could be expressed in those three little words.

Something moved outside and for all we knew, it

could be another drift of snow falling from the roof or the trees. I wouldn't even mind if we were stuck here a few more days.

"Wait." Levi sat up, pushed the blankets around me, cocooning me in, and jumped up. "Do you hear that?"

"I think it's bears and you should come back and snuggle by the fire some more until they leave." I knew it wasn't bears. Bears don't talk and there were several men's voices outside.

"Uncle Kingman? Is that you?" Levi ran to the door and yanked on it, trying to get it unstuck from the mounds of snow that had frozen around it overnight.

Normally, I would have been excited to jump up and join him. If there were people outside come to dig us out, that meant our secluded time together was over and real life would invade. Real life and I didn't get along that well. People just thought I was weird and most of my short relationships died the second we got out of the bedroom and into the light of day.

I didn't want that to happen this time. But I also wasn't going to pretend to be something I wasn't. Not when I'd felt so much joy and love being exactly who and what I was when I was with Levi last night.

Nope. I was going to make sure that didn't happen. Right now. "Hey, if your family is outside, you might want some pants."

I grabbed the soft furry Santa pants from his duffle bag and tossed them to him. Then I found my snuggly onesie jammies and pulled them on. Instead of helping get the door open, I tossed another couple of logs on the fire.

The power still wasn't back on and if we were digging out, it would get colder in here.

Levi stopped yanking on the door and came over to me. I couldn't look up at him. Our one night was over and I didn't want it to be. "Olive. Hey, look at me."

He grabbed my chin and cupped my face in both his hands, tipping my face up to his. "Tell me what's going through your head right now. Because it clearly isn't excitement for being rescued."

"I'm not very good at families and they aren't very good at me." He and I may be head over tails for each other, but in the light of day and reality, relationships weren't as easy as they were on bearskin rugs in front of a fire. But I had to believe this was real, that this was more than a crush and a one-night stand.

Levi and I saw each other, all the way down to our souls. I wasn't giving that up. But I was... scared of what the real world might do to that feeling we had.

Levi shook his head. "In the very unlikely circumstances that the Kingman's don't fall immediately in love with you like I did, then I will pile all the snow right back up in front of all the doors and windows and stay in here with you until the end of time."

Oh my heart. It's melting, it's melting. I squished my lips into a moue to keep from smiling too hard. "We'd starve."

He grinned down at me and stroked his thumb across my jaw. He had a twinkle in his eye that I couldn't help but smile at. "Surely Leadville has DoorDash or UberEATS. We can dig a pizza delivery snow shoot. It will be fine."

"Dude. What the hell are you two doing? We're going to be late for the Go Red Fun-raiser." A voice, and then a hand, and then a face that looked remarkably similar to Levi's popped through an opening in the snow at the top of the doorway. This must be one of the cousins.

"We're ready to go." Levi waved his hands in front of his Santa pants and my Christmas pajamas. "You guys are the ones who are late. What took you so long?"

The cousin laughed and in under five minutes the doorway was cleared and a whole slew of Kingman men all dressed as Santa, and one teenage girl dressed in blue with fur trim, stood in the living room of my tiny cabin. "How did you find us?"

"I had Levi send me his itinerary. I like to keep track of my family." An older man, who was quite the silver fox and must be the uncle Levi mentioned gave me a once over. "Your Aunt Verbena would be happy you were up here and taking care of her place now."

"You knew her?" I wished that I had.

"Yep. Levi's mother and I used to run errands for her in the summer when our family came up here on vacation. She used to feed us these great cookies that she was famous for. We called them Auntie's Ant cookies because she swore they were filled with ants and not chocolate chips. She used to have this place decorated in all kinds of ant paraphernalia. Pictures, and dishes, and various and sundry knick-knacks."

I touched the ant tattoo behind my ear. I'd had it done because before I'd been diagnosed with ADHD, it felt like there were ants running in and out of my brain all the time. I liked that it was also a tiny connection to the only family member I'd ever known of.

The teenager glanced between me and Levi. "You're practically already family, aren't you?"

Why did I have the distinct feeling she didn't mean because Levi's mom knew my aunt? Levi pulled me tight against his side, kissed the top of my head and said, "Yes, she is, Jules. Yes, she is."

I very much wanted to be a part of a family. Almost as much as I wanted to be with Levi. To get both would be far beyond anything I ever dreamed of.

"Uh, Uncle Levi, you might want to put a shirt on. It's like two degrees outside." Teenager wrinkled up her nose at him.

Levi winked at his young cousin. "Maybe, but I'll earn a lot more money for the American Heart Association with my shirt off, don't you thi--"

I smacked him right in the delicious abs, and snagged the red Santa shirt from the nearby bag and shoved it at him. "Those are my abs now, thank you very much. I shall not be sharing them, fundraiser or not."

Levi beamed down at me. "Yours, huh?"

"Yes. Mine." That was as much of an I love you as I was willing to say in front of all these people. But I real one would be forthcoming. Maybe when I took that Santa shirt and pants back off of him.

"Okay." He slipped the shirt over his head, waved his family out the door, and tugged me to go along too. "Then let's go raise some fun and some money. Then we'll come back here and figure out what to do about your house."

"Oh, am I coming with you?" My question had everyone turning around and staring at me.

His uncle leaned over and stage whispered to me, "He always did have ants in his pants, acting before thinking." He gave Levi that look that said get-your-shit-together. "You might try asking the girl to be your date, kid. Thought I taught you better how to treat women."

Levi swallowed hard enough his Adam's apple bobbed. "Yes, sir. You did."

He turned to me, brushed his lips across mine way to briefly, and then got down on one knee. "Olive, I know we've only known each other for a hot minute. Well, a very cold six-hundred or so minutes but I know. I absolutely know you're the one for me. Will you be my date to the Go Red for Women Christmas fun-raiser today, and then spend the rest of your days and nights with me too?"

The cousins went so silent, they might have frozen in the wintry morning air. No one even took a breath. Although the teenager, Jules, did smile at me and make big eyes that were encouraging my answer.

When you know, you know. It's not as crazy as it sounds when your brain goes a million times faster than everyone else's. I didn't need more time to think about it. "I love you, Levi. Let's do this."

"Yes!" Jules fist-pumped the air. "Another girl in the family."

Need more Cocky Kingmans who fall for the curvy girls?

Start the series with *The C*ck Down the Block* today!

ALSO BY AMY AWARD

THE COCKY KINGMANS

The C*ck Down The Block
The Wiener Across the Way
The P*ssy Next Door
The Anaconda Downstairs

ABOUT THE AUTHOR

Amy Award is a curvy girl who has a thing for football players, fuzzy-butt pets, and spicy romance novels. She believes that all bodies are beautiful and deserve their own love stories with Happy Ever Afters. Find her at AuthorAmyAward.com

Amy also writes curvy girl paranormal romances with dragons, wolves, demons, and vampires, as Aidy Award. If that's your jam, check those books out at AidyAward.com

www.ingramcontent.com/pod-product-compliance
Lightning Source LLC
Chambersburg PA
CBHW031236211125
35743CB00022B/72